RULER

Book Three of The First Plane Trilogy

PATTI LARSEN

Chapter One

The hunched and twisted little demon bent over, one unmarred hand clasping a glass vial of pale purple liquid. Sloshing accompanied a counterpoint of low moaning rising from the emaciated demon half-conscious on the slab bed. I held myself very still in the chill air of the cell as Portlish, the nectar cook, tipped the vial over Rameranselot's lips and allowed the thick stream to pour, mist swirling from the mouth of the bottle, between his parched lips.

My thick, black fingernails dug into the palms of my hands in the effort it took not to lunge forward and knock the cook aside, to protect the demon I loved from more torture. Because it was torture, plain and simple. Every dose of the newest attempt at an antidote Portlish tried to create ended in the same result—agony for Ram and utter failure.

And yet, I couldn't bring myself to lose hope. As Ruler of my people, I had to believe there was a way to save not only Ram, but all of the demons lost to the Planeless cult. The new breed of nectar created by their leader, Xeoniteridone, was being used to suppress demon power in order to allow their sorcery to arise. The cult leader's rapid success stripped me of the vast majority of my guards as well as put Demonicon at risk of utter failure. The sorcery the cult leader had access to rapidly disassembled the Node holding my world together, breaking it into its component planes, rendering it back to its original, fractured state. And there was very little I could do about it.

Without an antidote to the nectar, without the means to bring my demon subjects back into control of their elemental magic—and their minds—Demonicon was, ultimately, doomed. Not even my sister, Syd, saver of worlds and powerful maji, had been able to put a stop to the degradation. And the mighty drach, first race born of the Creator, were also stumped, my friend and ally, Mabel, as ineffective as the rest of us.

Yes, I'd managed to keep Xeoniteridone from severing one of the planes during an actual confrontation. But tracking him down in order to do so again was proving almost impossible. I'd tried a few times in the last thirty-six hours, chasing ghosts and shadows as he dipped into Demonicon from wherever he hid and stole another plane from me before I could even muster myself to follow. He'd learned not to face me directly, that much was clear. It might have been comforting to know I could defeat him one-on-one, but I had to find him first. Which meant he seemed determined to ensure we never had such a confrontation again.

At least, not until he knew he could defeat me. And leaving the next time and place to his discretion made me incredibly nervous.

My teeth ached from clenching them, hands almost numb from balling my fists as I waited for the inevitable. My mind might wander during these times of testing, but my focus remained with the pale and sweating demon stretched out on the cold stone slab, his precious face turned away from me. When he didn't react immediately to the dose, Portlish leaned back with a hopeful half-smile.

An expression which shifted to disappointment and frustration as the first convulsions took over Ram's body.

I wrapped my power around him, sorcery all that was available to me, though my grandmother's spirit still had full control of her own demon power. Ahbi stayed back, out of my way. She'd tried a few times to assist, and only seemed to make things worse, her magic drawing howls of pain from Ram. Instead, I soothed him with the blackness of my hungry energy, drawing out the agony into the dark as he writhed and tears streamed from the corners of his eyes.

For one moment, they flickered open as Ram's head tossed to the side, his gaze meeting mine. I barely recognized him, his sunken cheeks, pink skin once burnished red and deep-set eyes seeming to sink into his skull. But when our gazes met, I saw a flash in him, the note of recognition, and I finally did let hope swell inside me.

"Ram," I whispered, holding my ground, trembling from the effort.

"Meira," he croaked. I saw his throat working, knew he fought the control the nectar had over him, tried to say more. My feet moved without my permission, knees bending, my hands cupping his cheeks. Points of moisture landed on his face as my tears finally took over, and I crumpled under the weight of what was happening to him.

"Ram," I said. "Fight it. Please."

He gargled something, one hand rising in a whip-like motion, thinned fingers digging into the flesh of my arm. And then his eyes rolled back in his head, body arching upward, a seizure sending powerful tremors through his body. No amount of sorcery could ease his suffering, though I tried. When he finally collapsed, I was sobbing, caring less Portlish saw, nor that Ram's aunt, Zinnia, once my father's fiancée, watched with her own terrible sadness on her face.

"I'm sorry, Ruler," Portlish said in his velvet voice. "I don't know what I'm missing." His own frustration came through loud and clear, though I couldn't bring myself to feel sympathy for him. Still, I managed to hold back the snapping response I longed to throw at him, demanding a solution.

It wasn't Portlish's fault. And anger would solve nothing at this point.

I rose from the edge of Ram's stone slab bed, stepping away as he passed into troubled unconsciousness. Zinnia's hand caught mine as I stepped away, holding me there. Her clear gaze held too much empathy, far too much. She would make me cry all over again.

"Progress," she said. "He's never spoken before."

I glanced at Portlish who shrugged. "Perhaps," he said with a deep sigh. "Perhaps."

Hope whimpered in my heart and curled into a ball of defeat.

"No more," I said, voice shaking despite everything I did to keep it level. "He can't take any further testing."

Zinnia didn't comment, stroking her nephew's damp forehead with her free hand. Portlish didn't argue, either, though his next statement was obvious.

"I must have a subject to test," he said, tone low and apologetic. "I'm sorry."

I nodded brusquely, turning from Ram, wiping at the

tears on my face, the offensive things. "The next dose," I said, "you test on me."

"Ruler." Zinnia's disapproval did nothing to change my mind. "We've had this conversation."

"We have," I snapped at last, refusing to look at her. "Although you may think your Daeva leader has a right to tell me what to do, I will remind you I am still Ruler." Even if my own advisors agreed with them. As far as I was concerned, the secretive and meddling Daeva had no say in my decisions. They'd spent the last few millennia making sure no Ruler knew what they were up to. Until me. And now only because they were finally in over their heads and needed my help. I wasn't in a charitable mood when it came to Zinnia's order and didn't know if I'd ever be again.

"I need my power back," I said, the waver gone from my voice. A tidy lie, but not completely dishonest. I had access to demon magic through my grandmother, but I needed access and control over my own. And yet, my present upset was about Ram, and we all knew it. While finding a cure for him meant also finding one for me and all the other demons lost to Xeoniteridone and the Planeless cult, I was less worried about my people than the suffering figure on the slab before me. He moaned in time with my thoughts as I stepped forward and jabbed Portlish in one crooked shoulder with my finger. "Find the cure," I said. "And bring it directly to me when you're done."

Portlish bowed to me, gaze flickering to Zinnia before settling on me again. "I'm doing my best, my Ruler," he said, distress in his entire twisted body. "I swear I am."

"I know." I softened, patting the same spot I'd just prodded. "But we're running out of time." I really didn't need to state the obvious. Everyone around me knew just how imminent the fall of Demonicon was, even Portlish, mostly locked in the lab that had been Theridialis's. Not for the first time, I thought with regret about the old demon scientist and his loss, purportedly to the Planeless. I knew, with his help, we would have had a cure by now—most likely the reason he'd been kidnapped in the first place.

But he wasn't here, and Portlish, formerly a nectar street cook, was all I had.

I shuddered as I felt a sliver of the Node leave, so in tune with it through my sorcery I was aware of every single loss the moment it happened. Ahbi shivered inside me in echo to my reaction, though she remained silent as she had been over the last day and a half. I found I missed my grandmother's constant flow of chatter and, despite the struggles we'd faced finding balance between the two of us, wished she would at least be one thing in my life that felt normal.

Avenesequoia, one of my closest advisors and the sister to my beloved silver Persian/demon boy, Sassafras, poked her head in the doorway, face composed though I knew her heart was breaking for Ram from her refusal to look at him.

"Ruler," she said in her light voice. "Jabuticabron has returned."

I nodded to her, pausing one last moment to bend and press my lips to Ram's feverish brow. He muttered something I didn't catch before sighing and falling into a deeper sleep. His heart rate slowed, almost dangerously so, and I knew I was right to stop the testing. As strong as he was, Ram wouldn't survive much more of this, and his loss I would never accept.

Squaring myself for the world above the cell where he was held, I settled my Ruler persona around me and followed Sequoia out into the hall, the fear I'd return to find Ram gone forever rising with familiar agony even as my feet carried me away from him.

chapter two

The Seat felt empty, echoing and hollow. The vast
number of demons who cared for the ruling class and the
guards who protected us had fled, either to battle with the
Planeless or in fear for themselves and their families. In
their absence came a feeling of great emptiness. I had no
idea how much their presence influenced the solidity and
stability of the mountain until they were gone. So strange
to me, this vacuum, where once I was surrounded by
layers of demon power. The sense of them, their demon
souls, and the power they held had always been as familiar
to me as the polished rock beneath my feet.

The magic of the Seat itself remained, of course, and
filled some of the void left behind. But the absence of the
living, breathing pulse of the mountain, the demons
making up the day-to-day experience, no flow and ebb of
life, stirred sadness in me. It seemed more and more the

ruling Seat of Demonicon emptied of the living, leaving me to a towering spire of echoes and ghosts, only the court and their personal servants left behind. They, I knew, would never flee, clinging to the old ways as though they were a lifeline. So ironic, considering their disapproval of me, their supposed support of my father's attempt at demonocracy. It was obvious to me the family who made up the ruling class of Demonicon cared less for change and more for stirring trouble. I suppose I always knew that, though the sight of the court pretending things were normal in their fancy outfits and posing postures made me wish I could just shove them collectively over the side of the mountain.

The court didn't matter, their need to hold tight to what they knew, their refusal to openly admit they had a part in this disaster irrelevant. I would deal with them after this was over—and if I was unable, if Xeoniteridone did defeat me, they deserved each other.

As for the common demons serving the mountain, I had never felt their support in full, but the majority did not oppose me. They were more concerned with the needs of those they served and, now, the protection of their families to really care who sat on First Seat. I wished it was the ordinary demon on the street who had the most say in how our world was run. And grinned sadly to myself as I realized I was thinking like Dad.

Since it was his plan to democratize Demonicon that

got me into this giant pickle in the first place, I found it rather amusing I now swayed toward his way of thinking. But demons would never adapt to ruling themselves through election and debate. In our hearts, we were controlled by the need for power. I might have had the benefit of a witch mother to temper my desire to increase my magic, but I still possessed the monster inside who craved more and still more. Now I knew it was sorcery, it made much more sense. Still, that knowledge only solidified my understanding demons would only ever be antagonistic and greedy. Not exactly an ideal for demonocracy.

Still, I had to admit, the present system was sham and a disaster. So, I'd have to do something. I shook my head to myself as I walked the quiet hall to the elevator. Later. I didn't have time to worry about such things. Not when my world crumbled around me. Especially now, with Demonicon's end so near, reduced and fractured, the Seat itself reflecting the sudden quiet of the loss of all the souls that used to keep it running.

My platform boots sounded like thunder on the black stone floor as I stepped from the elevator and into the main corridor of my level, carrying me down the hall and to my double office doors.

Jabuticabron saluted as I entered, though I waved off his gesture with weariness and some irritation. The sight of a shining Persian cat sitting in the middle of my desk with his fluffy tail wrapped around his paws made me want to scoop Sassafras into my arms and hug him close, likely to weep all over again. Ram's predicament was now layered over with the emptiness of the Seat and my own feelings of failure, compounded by my total lack of anything resembling a plan moving forward. It was almost impossible to accept, but I was at a total loss as to what to do next, despite my absolute need to do something.

Instead of embracing my cat friend like a baby blanket and weeping my frustration into his fur, I spun and sat on the edge of my desk, arms firmly crossed over my chest to hold me together, if that was possible. So far, so good.

"Report," I said, not meaning to bark, but unable to speak softly for fear of losing it completely. I knew Jabut would forgive me.

He bowed abruptly and spoke. "I wish I had better news," he said, making my insides sag with further defeat. I had hoped he, at least, would offer me a glimmer of light to cling to. Only then did I see the weariness in the lines of his young face, how beaten and empty he seemed. I forced myself to remember I wasn't the only one suffering. But the spark of refusal in his gaze told me no matter how hard I tried to convince him to step down, he never would. And I refused to ruin him by using my Ruler position against him—such an act would, despite my best intentions, make him appear weak to those he led. Jabut, loyal to his last breath, slumped his shoulders forward a moment before physically jerking himself back into a stiff and formal position. "No matter what we do, how hard we fight, we are losing by the hour, my Ruler."

I nodded, accepting the spark of hope was a lie I told myself despite the fact I knew fighting back. This was nothing new and I honestly hated to send him out there, again and again, to face endless defeat against the Planeless. "So much for Xeoniteridone's declarations of peace and love."

Jabut shrugged as Sassafras snorted next to me.

"Peace and love my furry butt," the Persian snapped. "More like lie and cheat and steal until there's nothing left."

"The Planeless supporters have turned to violence," Jabut said. "The few guards I've managed to protect from the recruitment are little match for them. I was certain if we could capture Xeoniteridone or one of his people we could put an end to this." It would never work. If Mabel and I had been unsuccessful tracking Xeoniteridone, I didn't see how Jabut could manage it. And yet, I had to be seen doing something, and my guard captain seemed eager to try when I sent him out only two days ago. Had it been that long? It felt like only moments and yet, as though years had passed in a slowly spiraling downward turn to darkness.

I had no choice but to trust his enthusiasm to hand

some punishment back to the Planeless after all the damage Xeoniteridone and his people had inflicted so far. And so I sent my soldiers out into battle, fighting a war they could never win against an enemy who seemed to be invincible.

"There are far more of them than is possible," Jabut said. "We'll engage a small force only to find ourselves battling ten times that number and forced into retreat." His agitation was almost painful to watch. His broad shoulders twitched in time with a tic on his right cheek, winking his eye at me as his clenched fists shook. I guess I wasn't the only one who held in their anger that way.

"He must be bringing them in from other planes," I said. And sighed. It was a perfect strategy, really, worthy of a mastermind general. Wait for my forces to move in on a small bait target group and surround them with his own troops brought over from the planes he'd stolen from me. "That's it, then." I reached out and patted Jabut's arm. "You're to stand down, you hear me?" He opened his mouth to argue, but I shook my head. "Small forces only on the remaining planes." There were so few now, more leaving by the hour, it hardly seemed worth it, but I didn't want to leave them completely defenseless. Except doing so meant swelling Xeoniteridone's membership. I waffled back and forth on the order as I pressed on. "The rest pull back and protect Ostrogotho." We were the last bastion, the first plane to be tied to the

Node. And the ultimate goal of Xeoniteridone and his Planeless horde. Which meant, if we were to survive this, the capital of Demonicon had to stand.

Jabut's shoulders sagged again as he finally caved and nodded. "Yes, my Ruler." I hated seeing him so defeated. Sassafras slipped toward me, snuggling against my side as Sequoia joined her brother at last, putting an end to her distance, slipping under one of his arms. He hugged her with an absent expression.

"We're out of options," I said, Ahbi sighing heavily in my head. "We've tried everything and nothing has worked." How could things have fallen apart so very fast? "Our last hope is Portlish and the antidote."

And even that might not help, Ahbi sent, startling me as she spoke for the first time in what felt like forever. *Or it may come too late.*

"The drach?" Sequoia's worried gaze met mine. "There's nothing they can do?"

I shook my head, one hand stroking Sass's soft fur. His rumbling purr used to soothe me, backed by his empathetic magic gathered over his time with the Hayle coven. But no more. The sorcery in me only devoured it and asked for more. "Mabel is gone with Max and Syd," I said. "They confirmed the damage to the veil is tied to what Xeoniteridone is doing. Every piece of Demonicon he takes away increases the mess Syd's son, Gabriel, made years ago." The boy's talent, a physical gateway to the dark universe twin to ours, as well as all the planes on this one, was going to be a trial to control, and I felt glad he wasn't mine to watch over. "They have their claws full with holding the Universe together."

"I hate to say the word hopeless," Sass said. "But."

We all fell into glum silence.

No, Ahbi sent. *We will fight, to the last breath, the last moment. Until we can no longer. Hope has a funny way of giving you what you need as long as you don't forsake her.*

Sass grunted. "You're right," he said. "Thanks, Ahbi."

I stood, scooping him into my arms, still facing his siblings, closing the distance between us until we were in a tight circle. "No matter what happens," I said, choking up with emotion I could barely control, rising from the thinly controlled wall of composure I erected to protect me from completely losing it, "thank you for standing by me. It's been an honor and a privilege to have your faith and loyalty."

They murmured their answers, words I didn't hear over the pounding of defeat in my head.

chapter three

I looked out over my city from the balcony, hands gripping the stone railing so tightly it was a wonder neither my bones nor the stone cracked. While the initial mob-mentality meltdown on the streets seemed over, desperation and hopelessness radiated back to me from the quiet, almost deathly silence of Ostrogotho. The loss of the planes became quickly apparent and any attempt I made to calm the populace only made things worse.

My first try ended up in a massive show, one I now felt certain was planned by Xeoniteridone, in which a major plane was lost and an earthquake shook the city. It took all the guards I had to bring Ostrogotho to any semblance of order after that. As much as it pained me to do so, knowing there would be repercussions and backlash among common demons, I'd declared martial law. At least that way I could make sure everyone had enough food and water, while restricting movement as much as possible to keep the city—and its demons—intact.

Still, history was rarely kind to leaders who made their own people their enemy, even for the best of intentions, and I was on constant alert for a rebellion outside of one planned by the Planeless. All I needed was for a storm of angry demons to try to take the Seat. I needed them orderly and quiet, one less distraction.

With very few resources, I had no idea if my plans were working out, though Jabut assured me there were enough guards—at least now I'd pulled them from fighting the Planeless—to keep Ostrogotho running and marginally civilized. I knew he was keeping details of clashes from me. It was obvious on his wide, tanned-to-crimson face by the way he skimmed over my questions. But by that point, I didn't care anymore. It was his job to handle it, and I would do my best to stop worrying I was doing irreparable damage to my people.

But for how long? I unclenched my hands long enough to bring them down with solid thunks on the black stone. Time ticked away faster and faster, it seemed, as each of the planes separated one at a time and left me with terror growing in my heart.

Then again, why was I so worried? I leaned forward with a sigh, releasing my grip, resting my crossed arms on the rail. Demonicon was on the verge of collapse. And the demons of Ostrogotho, if Xeoniteridone had his way, wouldn't be mine to worry about for much longer.

So much gloom. I'd never felt so desperate, so out of control. Knowing there was nothing I could do to stop the end of my people made me want to curl into a ball under my covers and never come out. To be known as the last Ruler, the one who was the ruin of everything? Not the distinction I was looking for. And no matter the opinions of others, I truly cared for my people. How could I have let them down like this?

Enough of the self-flagellation, Ahbi sent, though softly and with kindness. *It serves no one.*

I flinched from her, knowing she was right, even as my eyes settled on a rising column of black smoke in the distance. I heard the rumble of dissention, knew my city was a volatile mix of terror and frustration waiting to explode.

I've failed them all, I sent back. *Grandmother, I'm not beating myself up. It's truth. Just plain truth.*

They've failed themselves, Ahbi sent. *Their need for power and their petty drive to be better than each other has prevented them from seeing the big picture until it was far too late.* She sighed deeply. *And that, my dear, isn't your fault, but evolution's.*

Regardless, I sent. *It's over, Grandmother.* I hadn't voiced it before, worried I'd fall apart when I did. But as I stood there, half a dozen suns setting in the west, a hand full of moons waiting to rise—all that remained of the planes of

Demonicon—my city cold and dark below me, I realized the acceptance of the truth was rather freeing. *We can't win. Demonicon is done.*

It is, Ahbi whispered. *But that doesn't mean the fight is over.*

I let my mind drift over her words. *You think there is a future for us after this is done?*

I do, she sent. *After all, Demonicon was made whole once before. Why can't we do it again?*

A ripple of shock slid through me. *You mean, let it go and then put it back together? I wouldn't even know where to start.* Not to mention if Demonicon was gone, that would mean Xeoniteridone in control and I was pretty sure he wouldn't just let me take control and piece the puzzle back together.

It's a possibility, Ahbi sent. *All endings have beginnings waiting to happen next, Meira. And this instance is no different. Perhaps Demonicon will never be one again. But something is coming.*

I actually took comfort from her words. The tight clench around my heart eased somewhat. *I'd rather it didn't come to that.*

Agreed, she sent. *But life goes on, with or without us, Meira.*

She sounded so sad, almost as if she had more to tell me. But we were both distracted from our conversation as the air overhead tore in a flash of power and a giant drach sailed through. Mabel was already settling, in human form, on the balcony beside me before the gash in the veil sealed shut.

I hugged her quickly, the comfort of her returned embrace adding to the softening in me Ahbi began. Being around Mabel made it easier to take the impending destruction of Demonicon.

The door to my room creaked, the soft pad of paws joining us as Sassafras leaped up to settle on the narrow ledge of the balcony rail. His amber eyes were the exact color of the darkening sky, the setting suns back-lighting his fur and making him seem more a demon than I was.

"Mabel," he said. "You're well?"

I released her as she bowed her head to him.

"I am," she said in her deep and powerful voice, as calm as ever. "Max agreed I should return to remain with Meira as the end of Demonicon draws closer."

Everyone knew the truth, then. "Any idea what we should expect?" I shivered and hugged myself this time, as a thin wind broke through the shielding around the balcony.

Mabel didn't answer that question. "You've stopped fighting," she said.

I nodded. "We're just losing guards to the cult." My hands tossed into the air as I let out some of my remaining frustration in that gesture. "Which means we're only feeding Xeoniteridone's army."

The veil overhead opened again, this time disgorging

a larger drach with a small figure on his back. I suppressed the need to sob at the sight of my sister as the pair dove for the balcony, Mabel stepping out of the way as they did. I really had to do something about my emotions being so close to the surface. Certainly no one would blame me, but this was no time to be weak.

Sassafras remained in place, his fur ruffling in the wind they generated as Max and Syd landed side-by-side, my sister's dark hair swinging in a thick ponytail behind her. She rubbed her hands over the thighs of her worn jeans, t-shirt dusty from some encounter, a smudge of gray on one pale cheek. But her deep blue eyes were clear and full of concern for me as she stepped forward and hugged me until I was breathless.

Love you, she sent. *We'll make this work.*

I kissed her cheek and let her go. *So I've been told.*

"Mabel said you've confirmed Xeoniteridone's activity is the cause of the problem in the veil?" I addressed Max who nodded slowly, bald head catching the last of the light glittering in his diamond eyes.

"Indeed," he rumbled in his massive voice, hands clasped before him. "Now that we know the true source, we've been able to keep the damage from spreading."

"But," I said, unable to stop my hands from clenching at my sides. The ache from my earlier abuse of them almost made me jump.

"But," Mabel said, her black hair swishing over the

stones at her feet, gray robe whispering as she raised both hands, "that is all we've managed to do."

"And doing so is taking all of our focus." Max didn't sound angry, just curious, as though he hadn't yet gotten over the shock of it all.

"Which means Demonicon is on its own still," I said. "Or what's left of it."

"Meems." Syd's distress showed on her face, the tightness of her shoulders, in her own fisted hands. "We can't help you." She shook her head, swiping at the smudge on her face, revealing a red mark evolving into a bruise. "Or Demonicon." Her hands fell again, tapping against her thighs in agitation. "I hate to say it, but—"

"You don't have to," I said, chin up, grateful Ahbi and I already had this conversation and the initial punch to the gut of loss was gone. "I already know Demonicon is doomed."

"So dramatic," Sassafras said, tail swishing. "We have no idea what will happen if the planes separate."

"I have to tell the court." The very least of things I looked forward to. They'd accepted me as Ruler again, despite the fact I had no access to my demon power or the magic of Demonicon, stolen away by my traitor grandfather, Henemordonin. Who had fled when Demonicon began to fall and I finally stood against him.

I couldn't think of him now, only hoped he died a slow and painful death on some distant plane. When this was over, maybe then I would go in search of him and show him just how big a mistake it was to cross me. If I was able. Until then, until this was done and Demonicon was no more, I had more important things to do than spend any more worry and anger on his waste of demonness.

Well said, Ahbi sent.

While the court willingly accepted me back when I first reappeared, their old arrogances and creeping need to bully and have their way was only exacerbating the issue. And I wasn't sure I could take another betrayal from them or even wanted to try to balance their increasing neediness in this time of crisis. If I'd learned one thing, it was the family of ruling class I was part of needed a firm and swift kick to their collective private parts, and if they pushed me any further, I knew just the chrome-tipped platform boot to do the job.

About five seconds before they had me stripped of power and dumped in the volcano at the center of the Seat. My hate for them was so powerful I shuddered from it and forced myself back to focus on my guests.

They must have seen my conflict, the struggle passing over my face, because even the drach, normally stoic and calm, looked faintly sympathetic. I cleared my throat and squared my shoulders.

"Want some backup?" For a moment, I wondered if Syd was listening in on my thoughts until I realized she was likely as passionate about a demon smackdown as I was, after her own run-ins with my grandfather and the court over the years. They'd bullied both of us in the past, judged and hated my sister and I for no reason except, perhaps, we were stronger than them, not pure demon but augmented by the witch magic of our mother. But Syd didn't have anything to worry about. She was maji, outside their ability to harm aside from a few harsh words and cold treatment. I had to live with these demons, day in, day out. They chose to put me back on the throne to save their sorry butts from a situation they helped create. I was supposed to do something, to act and make this all go away so they could return to their normal lives and not have to think about anything but fashion and who they could manipulate or take down in their next power battle.

Bubble bursting time was imminent. I was about to tell them exactly what they didn't want to hear. That Demonicon was about to fall and there was nothing anyone could do to prevent it.

Maybe if they had stood by me, had my back, supported me against Henemordonin. Granted me back the power I needed to destroy Xeoniteridone before he and his cult became a danger to us all. But my father, Haralthazar, gave them the means to blunt my power and my grandfather and the greedy demons who thought their personal quests for power were more important instead put us in this place, at this time, ready for the end.

I didn't fear them, not any longer. I held them, instead, in contempt. I'd been through far too much—from nectar addiction to betrayal to the loss of my power—to ever fear anyone again. But the confrontation itself I dreaded, if only because I'd had enough of their disapproval.

"I can handle it," I said. "They're not going to like it, but what's the worst that can happen?"

Syd's brow pulled together in sorrow as I turned away.

And ran right into Portlish.

chapter four

"My Ruler," he said, panting slightly as though he'd come to me in a great hurry.

I stepped back from him, half-turning to allow him to see I wasn't alone. He bobbed nods and stared with wide eyes at my sister and the drach before gulping down a breath of air.

"What is it?" Had he found a cure? At least we'd be able to save some of the demons. Who was I kidding? We might be able to save Ram.

But the little cook's face twisted into despair. "I'm sorry," he almost wailed the words, "I've failed you completely."

So, no hope at all, then. "It's all right," I said, and it really was. "None of this mess has gone the way we wanted it to."

He shook, he was so worked up, off-kilter form vibrating with regret, one bulging eye twisting away to showing the white. "There's something missing," he said, turning from me to pace a tight circle in a hobbling gate on his uneven legs. "Something I can't find, no matter what I do." Portlish faced me, tears now running down his cheeks, so upset by his lack of expertise he seemed close to sobbing. "It's driving me mad, my Ruler. I just can't do it." His hands covered his twisted face, shaking even more violently. In a moment of compassion I thought myself now incapable, I embraced him and let him cry on my shoulder.

"You've done all you can," I whispered, feeling my own cresting emotions ease and retreat as I offered him what I could of comfort. Odd how trying to make him feel better worked on my soul, too. "And I can ask for no more. Thank you for your service, Portlish. Your Ruler is very grateful."

He pulled free of me, shaking his head, angry now over the layers of frustrated sadness. "I need more information," he said, dashing the tears from his damaged face with his perfect hands. "I need help."

"There is no help coming," I said as gently as I could, acceptance a warm and comforting ball in the bit of my stomach. Who would have known giving in to the truth would set me free of my fear and anxiety?

"My father," Sassafras said, voice grim, triggering an

old hope I thought lost. "He's the only one who can figure this out, Meira."

Theridialis. Hadn't I just thought of him, down there in the cell where my love was fading from me with every attempt to save him? But we'd searched, unable to locate the old scientist, that particular hope dead and gone. I could only guess he'd been taken to one of the severed planes, held captive or, perhaps, turned. But I couldn't bring myself to believe he'd been converted, not with the fight he'd put up when they'd come for him. He'd left his own lab in shambles. If he'd become one of the Planeless converts, he would have simply gone with them happily. I'd seen it happen myself.

Which meant—I allowed the old hope to rise again—Theridialis had found a cure himself, the very reason he was taken and why by force. They'd been unable to coerce or turn him.

I couldn't allow such thoughts, I just couldn't. I'd been here before, so many times. Round and round, more and more frustrating. I glared at Sassafras who glared right back. "We've been down this road," I said. "With about as much luck as we've had with anything surrounding this disaster."

"We've had our focus splintered until now," Sass said, glowing eyes points of light in the dark sky as the suns disappeared at last. "Because of our need to hold Demonicon together. But if we can pour all of our resources into finding him, we may be more fortunate."

It really wasn't a bad plan, for all that. And would give me something to do while I waited for the end. Considering it was the best plan any of us had, I couldn't really turn Sass down. Syd reached out and stroked his fur, her eyes never leaving mine.

"All right," I said, seeing his eagerness wake, feeling my own stirring need to act, a sensation I didn't think I'd feel again. "We'll track down Theridialis and hope he's not converted. And that he has an antidote. And that we're not too late." It was hard not to roll my eyes at my own words. "If. And. But."

Sass snorted. "So little faith," he said.

"Not much to hang faith on these days," I said.

Max tensed suddenly, head up, eyes on the rising moons though I was certain his mind ranged much further. When his gaze dropped, he seemed tense, nervous, a big concession from the steady drach leader.

"We have to go." He gestured to Syd who wavered a moment before nodding. She kissed Sassafras then came to my side.

One more hug from my sister and she and Max were on the balcony railing. I noticed she didn't look over the edge as the giant drach launched himself into the air, morphing into his dragon shape while she waited for him to finish. It made me wonder if she still fought her fear of heights, a fear triggered right here on Demonicon, so many years ago.

"Keep us posted," she said.

I waved at her, a half-hearted gesture, almost echoing her sentiment, but not bothering. Neither of us were able to do anything about the other's predicament anyway.

Cold darkness brushed past me as I turned back to Portlish. Bakari, the quiet and dangerous agent of the Daeva, bowed his head to me, appearing from out of nowhere in his signature manner, while Zinnia slipped through the balcony doors to join us.

"Pagomaris is with Ram," she said in a hurried voice. I'd only just discovered my trusted aide—a servant to Ahbi for centuries—was also one of the secret order. We had to leave one of them with Ram—also a member—at all times to make sure he didn't hurt himself. Only sorcery could contain him when his craving for nectar drove him to the edge of madness. I could trust Pagomaris to keep him asleep and away from any harmful outbursts. At least, for now.

"We're shifting our focus," I said, the leader in me taking over naturally, confidence appearing from the ether despite the fact this new plan would likely fail, too. But it felt good to have something to fixate on, I had to admit. And thank Sassafras for the subject of that plan. "I've pulled back all guards to Ostrogotho." Bakari looked like he wanted to argue. Or punch me in the face. Either way, I forged on, and he remained silent. "Our last hope is Theridialis. We need to find him and, if we can, finish the antidote."

"You will allow Demonicon to crumble?" Bakari's gravelly tone cut like a blade. There was a time I feared him or, at least, didn't think I could trust him. But I had grown thick armor in the last few weeks, not to mention a healthy dose of irritation toward him and his order, and instead of allowing him to hurt or intimidate me, I hit him with sorcery and tightened my grip.

I was so done with being bullied, intimidated and pushed around.

"I'm doing what I can," I said, quiet, calm as he struggled with me, "against impossible odds and a situation brought on by centuries of mistrust and idiocy." He must have gotten the reference to his own people's lack of assistance because his stony face fell from anger to blank and he stopped fighting. I released him from my grasp, resuming the conversation. "Now, if Theridialis has been taken to another plane and is being held there, what resources or options do we have to find him?"

Someone cleared their throat, soft and hesitant. I gestured to Sequoia who held out pages of notes. "I'm not sure if this helps to locate Father," she said with a hint of excitement, "but I've been piecing together what I can of his work since his capture." She shook the pages, some crisped and almost burned beyond recognition. But as she moved them, amber fire raced over the surface, words and scribbles and markings showing clearly in lines of writing embedded by demon magic. "It took some doing, but I've fit the pieces together."

"You have the cure?" Portlish reached for the pages himself, eagerness replacing his anxiety.

"No," Sequoia said, gently handing them to the cook. "But I'm now certain Father had an antidote before he was captured."

That was one question answered—and meant finding Theridialis was even more important. No longer a hope or a thin thread of possibility. If he really had come up with a cure, we should have been pursuing his location more aggressively all along. I was an idiot to let it go.

What did I say about beating yourself silly? Ahbi's soft correction pulled me back from the brink of guilt. *We're going to look for him now. That's all we can think about. Now.*

Easy for you to say, I sighed at her. *And since when did you become so nonchalant and unaccusing?*

Since I realized none of it matters in the face of the end, she sent. *Meira, I may have ruled Demonicon for longer than I should have, but you've been confronted with more trials and pain than I ever was. It's altered my perspective. And made me appreciate the here and now.*

Fair enough, I sent. *Here and now it is. I'll leave it up to you to keep me on the narrow.*

My pleasure, she sent. Hesitated. *I'm proud of you.* She pulled back from me, falling silent, leaving me with mixed feelings drawn from sadness and gratitude.

I realized then everyone stared at me, waiting for me to continue. They must have known I was talking to Ahbi, because they didn't seem distressed, just watchful.

"If we can find him," I said, "we can at least stop the spread of the nectar in Ostrogotho. Demonicon may fall, but this plane will remain safe and protected from Xeoniteridone and his cult." It wasn't much, but I'd take it. Until the full cult marched on my city. But I'd deal with the army of the Planeless if and when they showed up to take Ostrogotho from me.

"If it works," Sass said, tail now thrashing as he hopped down from the railing, "we can find a way to distribute it to the other planes, as well. Demonicon might be gone, but at least demons will have a fighting chance to pick up the pieces on their own planes."

It wasn't a perfect solution, but it felt like progress and hope woke again. I just hoped this kernel of positive thinking wasn't about to die a slow and painful death like all the other ideas that had fallen victim to the Planeless. Only one way to find out, and I was a far cry from giving up when I had something I could do.

chapter five

My feet were heavy under me despite the spark of possibility the conversation on the balcony gave me. There were so many ifs, buts, and maybes in our plan, the core spark of it was smothered as I strode up the aisle in the midst of the family toward my throne. I almost snarled at them for their attention to detail, the elaborate costumes even more over the top than usual, as if dressing like idiots would make everything go away. Piles of fur and feathers and silver studding turned them into a sea of ridiculous, a caricature of demonhood. They were pathetic and clinging to their superiority if only through the way they dressed.

I, myself, had long given up on the pomp of court, my favorite skin-tight black cat suit under a shimmering robe of crystal-covered mesh the best I could muster. My only concessions to style were my chrome platform boots, a favorite gift from Syd. Even my long, curly hair hung mostly loose around me, clasped with a simple silver circlet at the nape of my neck, much as Mabel wore hers. It wasn't a conscious choice to buck the system, but I was tired of the charade, the make-believe and the falseness that went with the court's need to show the world they were better through elaborate costuming and pretentiousness.

My boots rang on stone as the court watched in silence, their usual whispering non-existent, for once. Perhaps they sensed what I was about to tell them. I'd been expecting the usual push back, the nudge of arrogance, the subtle—and not-so-subtle—challenges to my decisions. It was so uncharacteristic of them to stand there in their foolish attire and watch me with pinched faces, I could only guess rumor had traveled. It seemed Jabuticabron's orders to the guards to withdraw to Ostrogotho had made the rounds.

Oddly, I missed their antagonism and felt their sudden fear-fed apathy sap my energy. I forced it off, a clinging leech of need pushed against me. Ahbi did her best to block them while my sorcery begged to sip of their sweetness. With a spin of flourish to hide the intense battle going on inside me, I sank to my throne, my butt hitting the soft cushion of power Ahbi created for me as I faced the family. A soft titter of nervousness passed through them, their anxiety palpable in the air though not one of them spoke. I allowed the silence to stretch for a long moment as I observed them with what I hoped was a cold and stony demeanor.

"Your Ruler speaks," I said, hating the echo of their voices as they murmured back to me, with a passion so violent I quivered inside.

"We hear you, our Ruler."

Did they really? Liars, all of them. They never seemed to in the past, preferring to listen to the sound of their own voices, focus on the drives of their own black souls.

Kindly, Ahbi sent. *They've been arrogant asses all along. But they are afraid and you are their beacon.* I clenched my stomach against the truth, seeing she was right. They had finally arrived at terror, abandoned their arrogance once and for all. The worst possible timing, in my opinion. It would make what I was about to do all the harder. Would they panic? Cause a giant scene? At least in this state, I didn't think they would be able to muster the courage to try to have me killed.

Small miracles I would take and cherish.

I'd rather be anywhere but here, I snarled back, irritation at their lack of spine drowning me in anger.

Really? She sounded amused. *Really, Meira. Why don't I believe you?*

I grumbled back at her even as I sighed internally, my temper falling away as I absorbed what she said. And admitted to myself there was no other place I could be at this moment. *You're right*, I sent. *No matter how bad things get, I'm Ruler.*

And a Hayle, Ahbi sent. *Who never backs down from anything. Or trusts anyone else to do the dirty work necessary.*

I cursed her, my mother, and my sister even as a tiny smile won. *Oh, shut up*, I sent with amusement in my mental voice, grateful she defused me at last.

Ahbi laughed at me. *Your command, Ruler.*

It shouldn't have been funny, but it was. Because my grandmother was right. As I looked out over the gathered court, the darkness of the sky above visible through the clear shielding keeping us safe from the open air above, I realized I wouldn't want to be anywhere else. That this was my place, where I belonged, and no one was going to take it from me without a fight to the death.

My sorcery blossomed further under my family's acute attention, begging me to feed. I struggled against it a moment, shocked by the force of it as it tried to use them for sustenance, seeing their weakness even more clearly than I did. Syd never mentioned fighting hers, not like this.

Syd has other egos to help her and full access to her power, Ahbi sent, all traces of humor gone. *And you've been addicted to nectar.*

I slammed a wall up between me and the court, my body going rigid. While it would have been most satisfying to feed on them, I knew better than to go there. I wouldn't be a tyrant, not the uncontrolled girl my grandfather convinced them I was. Didn't mean they didn't deserve it, though. *Thanks for the reminder*, I sent.

Had the nectar made me more vulnerable? My sorcery retreated at last, though I could feel it burning beneath me, black flames licking at me, starving for food all of a sudden. The near-instantaneous awakening frightened me and convinced me more than anything I needed a cure so I could access my demon power to control the hunger of my sorcery.

I shook myself, but not before a wave of fear passed over the court. It was hard not to sneer at them, shove them aside, drain them as my sorcery wanted me to. What good were they, after all?

"How far my Demonicon has fallen."

My head jerked up, eyes bulging as a familiar figure strode with utter confidence down the aisle toward me. How did my grandfather manage to sneak in here? I'd ordered him instantly arrested if he ever dared showed his face after betraying us all to the Planeless.

Sorcery, Ahbi hissed as Henemordonin's scowling face made me want to leap on him with physical violence, left hand twitching toward the Second Seat, empty of his unwelcome ass.

"You dare show your face here, traitor," I snarled, gesturing to the guards. Jabuticabron marched forward with some of his men, but my grandfather, my former Second Seat and self-proclaimed Ruler of Demonicon, held up both hands, coming to a halt before me, the power of our planes wrapped around him in a visible show. He did it on purpose, of course he did, to remind the court just who held the magic to rule them.

And it wasn't me.

"Henemordonin," I said, voice shaking, barely able to contain my rage as the black flames rose again, blotting out everything, "you are under arrest for betraying everything Demonicon stands for." He I would have no trouble feeding from until he was a smear of dust on the floor before me. My rage blurred everything, took away my reason as Ahbi yelled at me to hold it together.

"Have I?" He pressed one hand to his chest, tone light, face hurt and offended. His silver beard bristled, giant body towering over most of the court as they looked at him with hope. What the hell was wrong with them? "I, who have done nothing but try to save our world from your incompetence."

My. Incomp—

He's playing you, Ahbi sent in a sharp jab of anger. *Kill him now, don't let him talk any further or all is lost.*

I gathered my power, ready to crush him, the darkness now welcome as it eagerly reached out to suck him dry.

Henemordonin's hand rose, one finger pointing at me

as my sorcery hit the wall of shielding around him. "Behold!" His words boomed around the throne room. "Your Ruler is a sorcerer."

They knew that already. And, as a matter of fact, so was he. I felt his darkness holding me back. But he wasn't done speaking as the court stared, wavered, fell under his spell as they always seemed to do.

They stared at me with guilty eyes and fear in their faces while my grandfather went on and my hate for them built to a fever pitch.

"She must be the enemy," he said, approaching with heavy steps, "in league with the Planeless. And you," he spun, still pointing, arm sweeping across in front of him, accusing the family as his words accused them, "believed her," he roared the words, "over your true Ruler." The power of Demonicon crackled and snarled, fighting him still. I wished I could take it back from him, but all my sorcerous side wanted to do was swallow it whole. And I had no idea if taking it would simply negate the full magic of my home thanks to the influence of the nectar I still suffered. Too risky, by far.

He turned back to me, face crinkled with faint disdain, though his tone never changed from the heavy, judging pressure so familiar to me now. I felt it press on me and shrugged it off, disgust at the gathered court's failings growing by the moment as my hate coalesced into utter apathy toward them.

They didn't deserve me.

No, they don't, Ahbi sighed. *They've earned your grandfather.*

"Tell us, oh false one," Henemordonin said. "What grand pronouncement were you about to make before I returned to seize my throne from your wickedness?"

He knew. I could see it in his eyes. Did he still have spies with eyes on me? No, I doubted it. The answer was, to any reasonable intellect, obvious.

I had to try deflection. "Where have you been all this time, Henemordonin, if you are as innocent as you claim?" The court barely reacted to my question. They didn't care, despite knowing he'd betrayed them. I suppose it was his word against mine, at this point, since I had no proof.

If they couldn't care less, why should I?

He was too much a practiced diplomat to allow me to steal his means to return. "Gathering evidence against you," he said. "Now, answer me, Senne. Answer *us*." He gestured to the watching demons.

It was impossible to muster emotion as I spoke in a dead and bored voice, no longer able to muster any kind of passion for the throne, for the watching court before me. I knew, before I opened my mouth and spoke, the corner he'd painted, the time he'd spent manipulating and convincing them of his perfection. That with the truth I had to offer, I was signing my own final moments as

Ruler. But I had nothing else to say and no will to try to fight any longer. They wanted Henemordonin? They were blind enough to accept his lies and deceptions? Then they could have him and he them, and I wished them only suffering and endless agony together.

"The end is near," I said as they moaned in time with my admission, swaying toward my grandfather's waiting magic. "I have done everything I can to save Demonicon. But, barring a miracle, it will all be over soon enough."

He spun on them, then, arms wide, the kindly, sad smile of their savior on his face. His speech was unnecessary. They were his, completely and utterly. Why had I even bothered to try to save them? Didn't stop Henemordonin from rubbing salt into my gaping wounds. "You heard her," he said. "She has given up on us, and worse, given us up to the evil threatening to destroy our world." It was an impressive performance, wasted. I felt their apathy, the failure of even the court's ability to care any longer, lost with my own caring, I supposed. They had quit long before I had, hanging their hopes, as thin as they were, on me. And now, here was Henemordonin, finishing me off as he always did. And they could barely bring themselves to raise a whisper of condemnation.

He might have won, but it was a hollow victory. There was no vitriol, no secret conversations muttered in my direction. Not a scrap of blame or emotional dedication. Just despair and loss and complete giving in to him, if only because he seemed, as always, stronger than me.

Henemordonin must have felt it, too, because as he turned to me, he seemed troubled. But instead of calling off this farce, he gestured at me one last time.

"I am the true Ruler of Demonicon," he boomed.

"What's left of it," I said, soft but carrying.

His scowl rippled over his face. "Does any challenge me?"

Pin drop moment. I saw my friends watching from the sidelines, Sassafras perched anxiously in his sister's arms, waiting for me to act. Even Mabel held her ground, though I could tell from the way her huge body swayed she wanted to come to my aid.

I chose to ignore them, even when Jabut's shoulders sagged for the last time, Sequoia's mouth covered with her one free hand as tears glistened in her eyes. No way was I dragging them into this final defeat.

Let him take the throne, I sent to my friends. *It doesn't matter anymore.*

Henemordonin's chest puffed as he faced no opposition. "Arrest her," he said. "And hold her for trial. The charge is betrayal by their Ruler of every single demon soul."

I stood as Rutorith came forward, patched eye crinkled as he scowled at my grandfather. His loyal guard seemed much less sure of himself these days. His hesitation gave me a flare of relief not all here were follow-the-leader fanatics with no minds of their own. But he was a soldier, and he had his orders, didn't he?

I forgave him, though, my hate for the court dying out in the face of this noble old guard who saw the way of things and wished he could act differently. But no way was I waiting for him to escort me from my throne. Instead, I descended two steps, still standing above my grandfather and the court. I paused, then, and nodded to the gathered family.

"I've tried so hard," I said, without judgment or anger, both emotions dead within me. "And you've cut me down at every turn." Henemordonin's face darkened as I shrugged. "Whatever happens from here, the fate of Demonicon is on you."

Rutorith didn't touch me as I strode past him, surrounded by guards as a handful held off my friends.

I'll be fine, I sent to them, striding past the weary and broken court. *Please protect each other and get out of here if you can.*

I will free you, Mabel sent, a fierceness in her voice I'd never heard before.

No, I sent. *You won't. The plan stands.* I turned my head slightly and nodded to them before continuing to the elevator, surrounded by guards. *I can take care of myself. Your job is to find Theridialis.* The platform bobbed under me as I stepped on board and spun to face the throne room, the elevator filling with giant demons at arms. *Nothing else matters now.*

They watched me as the platform descended, carrying me out of sight.

chapter six

The chill air was familiar, the feeling of the cold slab under me carrying ice to my veins. I shivered in the damp, the thin clothing I wore no match for the underground beneath the Seat. It made me think of Syd, the dark and damp little stone room, how she'd ended up here herself after being accused of killing Ahbi. Of course, that was a long time ago and the real murderer, Ameline Benoit, was dead. And yet, I found myself wondering if Syd felt trapped the way I did. If her temper had ruled her or if she felt as calm as I did, knowing they couldn't hold her even if they tried.

I was grateful Rutorith chose a different level than the one I was accustomed to visiting. My cell was on a lower level than where we held Ram, keeping him out of harm's way, at least for now. But, for the first time, I thought of his precarious situation and suddenly worried what would happen to him and Portlish if Henemordonin found them.

You know what he'll do, Ahbi sent, as calm and cold as I was. *He'll return Ram, and probably Portlish, to Xeoniteridone for re-inoculation and they'll both be lost to us.*

We can only assume he knows Ram is here, I sent. The urge to pace almost broke through my level calm. I'd never felt so relaxed and still, despite the cold, the need to get up and march out my frustration fading as fast as it appeared. How could I be so level headed at a time like this?

Ram will be fine, Ahbi sent, blunt, to the point. *Or he won't. We can't worry about him, now. And if Portlish is correct, if he's done all he can for us, his loss means as much as Ram's.*

Cold hearted, but very true. I bobbed a nod into the near-dark, the only light coming through the small, grated widow at the top of the heavy, metal door. My toes just touched the stone floor beneath me. The scent of mildew and dust tickled my nose, burned my eyes while I blinked away the desire to sneeze.

To the deepest bowels of the Seat with them, Ahbi sent in the same deadened tone. *Let them all suffer and die after Xeoniteridone converts them to his perverted need. You were right to give up on them at last. I'm so done with those ungrateful assholes.*

I ducked my head in another agreeing movement. *We've done all we can for the court*, I sent. *It's time to worry about us and let them burn.*

Ahbi hesitated. *Do we really feel that way?*

I shrugged. *Shouldn't we?* It felt good not to feel anything but this quiet acceptance. *We gave them all we had, and they've turned on us one more time.*

Agreed. Ahbi's mind shivered inside me. *Your grandfather was right about one thing. How far we have fallen.*

Well, it was no use just sitting here. Time to do something about escape, so I could help in the search for Theridialis. Being a fugitive didn't bother me all that much. I was a hunted demon, no matter what my circumstances. I suppose I should have been grateful Xeoniteridone was too busy with his takeover of my world to send more kidnappers after me. Sorcery could cut through even the most intense and ancient demon shields, something I learned when Zinnia saved me from my cousin and her Planeless friends showing up in my bedroom in the middle of the night.

Maybe now he knew I had access to my own sorcery, he saw no benefit in trying it. After all, I had the power I needed now to counter any attack he sent my way. And he knew, or thought he knew, how strong I was. I really hoped at this point it would come down to some kind of final confrontation between us so I could show him just how wrong he was about the mass of magic I had at my command.

Could be being booted from First Seat yet again was a good thing after all. It would make my life much easier working without having to consider my every move was being contemplated, each and every order given dissected and criticized. And since the court didn't seem to care if things fell apart as long as the demon with the best story was at the helm, I was now free to act as I needed to.

Comforting, the lies I told myself. But doing so helped to free me from the cold calm holding me down, pinning me with apathy. A fire woke inside me again, stirring Ahbi at the same time.

Ready to get the hell out of here? I hugged her magic quickly.

When you are, she sent. *So ready.*

First things first. I needed information and back up, just in case. I reached out for Syd, the natural first choice, using my sorcery to its limits. But the inevitable shield stood in my way. So easy to feel the multiple powers behind it, that it wasn't Henemordonin's strength holding me back, but that of the Planeless. No amount of wriggling or fighting could cut through it.

She'll come anyway, Ahbi sent. *The others will let her know and she'll rain fire and brimstone down on his royal ugliness.*

If they can reach her, I sent, shifting on the cold stone, hissing softly at the chill as I did. Ahbi's attempt to create warmth with her magic was smothered and devoured so quickly she swore and pulled back.

You know, Ahbi sent, *my power might not be useful, but yours is at full strength, correct?*

I've been trying to cut through, I sent. *No luck.*

Silly girl, Ahbi sent. *Not cut through. Escape.*

She showed me an image of a black hole, and I rolled my eyes at myself instantly, a grin breaking over my face.

That is, I sent, *if I want to escape.* Which, of course, I did. But teasing her seemed to fit the moment perfectly.

You'd rather sit here and catch a cold while your grandfather prepares to strip all your power? Ahbi's tone was so reasonable I laughed out loud.

Since you put it that way. I stood, shaking out my legs, my hands, stiff from the cold. *Now, since neither of us has done this before, maybe you'd like to tell me what I need to do?*

I was thinking about that, she sent. *Remember your test with the veil?*

I nodded. *We couldn't break through.* It had frustrated me at the time, knowing Syd accomplished what she called riding the veil easily. I was, of course, able to create a hole between planes, to carry me back to Wilding Springs when I wanted. And Ahbi mentioned she and some other demons she knew long ago were able to do the same on Demonicon itself. But the act had been forbidden for centuries, supposedly tied to the fragility of the Node. Now I wondered if it was really to protect demons from uncovering their sorcery somehow.

But we almost managed it, Ahbi sent. *And I'm certain, given the right combination of magicks, you would be able to travel inside this plane with only your witch and demon powers to aid you. But when it comes to riding the veil, I'm thinking something was missing. The key ingredient Syd uses to travel.*

That struck me almost like a blow. *Sorcery?*

It makes sense, Ahbi sent. *After all, we now know the veil is tied to it as much as any other magic. Which makes it logical you would need it to travel through.*

But Syd didn't have access to her sorcery when she started riding it, I sent. *She only had her witch and demon power, like me.*

But not like you. Separate, remember? Ahbi's mind churned inside mine. *She's never really been whole, always fragmented. Demon, witch, Sidhe, vampire. And sorcery.* My grandmother shifted slightly, her magic sighing. *She may not have known she had access, at the time, but I highly doubt her sorcery was completely inactive with all that magic activity going on in her body.*

A soft grunt escaped me. *Grandmother,* I sent, *you are brilliant.*

Happy to serve, she laughed. *Now focus. We don't have all day.*

As I reached for my power, I realized she was right. The echoing sound of feet approaching at a run finally broke through my apathy and drove me to act. Sorcery rumbled to life around me, the black flames licking at my skin while Ahbi focused her demon power into it.

There, she sent. *You feel it?*

The veil was right there, so real and alive I could almost touch it with my fingertips, much more so than when I'd tried last. I jerked my hands apart, tearing open a gaping black hole edged in the fire of Demonicon.

Too late, I turned as the heavy metal door clanged open.

And Portlish staggered through, supporting a weak, but wide-awake Rameranselot.

"Quickly, Ruler!" The crooked cook shoved Ram toward me, the demon wavering on shuffling feet as Portlish spun and slammed the door to the sound of heavy boots running our way. "You have to go, now!"

I met Ram's amber eyes, saw his pain, but felt him, the real him, knew it was him looking back at me.

"Meira," he whispered, still hoarse.

"Your support gave me hope. I tried one last time." Portlish grinned at me, an edge of excitement in his velvet voice. "It didn't do the full job, but he's no longer brainwashed." A heavy weight slammed against the door, interrupting his enthusiasm. Portlish squeaked once as the portal bounced from the impact. "You can trust him. But you have to get out of here before they find him!"

I held Ram up as he half-collapsed before catching himself again. "Come with us."

"I'll be fine," Portlish said. "Get Ram to Theridialis. If he doesn't have a cure, he will when he examines him."

That was enough for me.

"Open the door at once," the booming sound of Rutorith's voice ricocheting around the cell. "In the name of Ruler."

I spun with Ram as the door bounced again, gasped at the sight of Bakari stepping from the empty air to wait for me.

"You should know I would never leave you alone," he said before hefting Ram out of my arms. "After you."

I glanced back one last time at Portlish as the door finally gave under the pressure of Rutorith and his guards. It was so hard to leave the small cook behind, and I almost went back for him. My eyes lifted as I started to move and met those of the one demon I never expected to see here, not now.

Seeing the lean, handsome son of Xeoniteridone at the entry to my cell almost broke me. Flashes of memory as fast as strokes of high-powered lightning hit me over and over as the world stood still and our eyes locked. Lies, deceit, heartbreak and betrayal, all in one package I once considered a possible mate. I now burned with only hatred for him, the most powerful I'd ever felt for anyone.

Time snapped back into place to the roaring sound of Rutorith ordering me to stop. I wasn't paying attention, not to anything but the slim demon before me. Elphremantic lunged for me, face twisted in rage and his own brand of hate, ugly, dark, sickening. I shrieked like an animal, surging forward to meet him, to grasp him in my bare hands and tear him into tiny, bite-sized pieces dripping blood. He woke my emotion, my anger and frustration so much I threw all thought away and dove for the demon who pretended to care for me, who almost made me betray Ram.

Who fooled me into nearly giving my heart to another.

Bakari was much faster than I and, perhaps, was prepared for my reaction to the sight of Xconiteridone's son coming toward me. The assassin's hand snaked out and grasped my wrist and, with more strength than I'd felt even from my drach friend, Mabel, he jerked me forward and into the gap, plunging me into the veil while I screamed my fury into the darkness.

CHAPTER SEVEN

I stumbled out of the veil and onto cold stone, a familiar triad of elderly demons watching as I caught myself and spun on Bakari.

"WHY?" I lunged for him, pounding on his chest with my fists, sending him stumbling back under Ram's weight, unable to stop me from assaulting him. "I could have killed him. You should have left me to kill him!" Elphremantic's face wavered in my rage-filled memory, the flames of my sorcery striking out against Bakari.

"Ruler." Raethnn's soft voice carried power as the old demon leader of the Daeva's magic wrapped around mine in a surge and contained it. Or tried to. I was much stronger than her, a fact that seemed to shock her as I spun on her this time. But despite her weakness, her act succeeded anyway. I felt my anger cool as Ahbi soothed me, the hate I felt for Elphremantic rolling into the same emotion for the court, for my grandfather, for all the betrayal I'd suffered fading into a simmering pot of vengeance I just had to find a way to fulfill.

"Your safety and that of Rameranselot," Raethnn gestured at Ram held in his father's arms, "was more important than the death of a single demon, no matter how much he deserved to die."

The air beside me actually bellowed as a giant tear appeared and the massive drach form of Mabel burst through. She settled to the ground, wings outspread, fanning a great wind over all of us as she roared her own fury into the chamber. I clasped my hands over my ears as her voice echoed and bounced from one corner to the other, though my insides quivered with gratitude at her arrival. I knew I'd told her to leave me, to focus on Theridialis, but I had a feeling if I hadn't escaped when I did, she would have ignored my request and come after me anyway.

When she finally stopped her tirade of sound, I shook my head, working my jaw to massage my ear drums while she transformed into human shape.

I'd never seen her so furious, never seen any of the drach show such anger, as she swept toward me and gathered me to her, giant hands holding me firmly against her body.

"I'm okay." I hugged her, letting her feel my grateful joy at her arrival. "Mabel, I'm fine, honest."

Diamond eyes flared with multi-colored fire. "You are," she boomed. "And you will remain so or I will destroy this place myself."

I was so stunned by her continuing show of emotion, I almost missed it when Syd, Sassafras vibrating in her arms, arrived a moment later with the human-form Max. Only the touch of her sorcery alerted me, turning me around, still held in Mabel's hands. It was comical, honestly, to see the fear on the Daeva's faces, how Raethnn's pale pink skin turned almost white, eyes bulging as she stared at Mabel. Knowing the drach were powerful, the first race, was one thing. Seeing one of them truly angry? That was quite another. I was just glad Mabel was firmly on my side of the fence.

"Thanks for the rescue," I said to the Daeva leader, doing my best to diffuse the situation though a part of me was enjoying their fear. And it wasn't like they deserved any thanks. I'd managed on my own just fine, hadn't I?

Because I'm useless and uninformative, Ahbi said with a dry cut to her voice.

I hugged her with a mental laugh. *Goes without saying.*

Just placate the masses and let's move on, she sent, clearly amused.

The fear in the Daeva hadn't lessened much and, as I considered their state of mind, I shrugged to myself. I'd spent enough of my time in the last four years anxious and worked up. Served them right to have a dose of their own medicine. Instead of spending my energy on them, I waved at my sister with a little grin.

"Hey, Syd. What's up?"

Her angry expression softened, worry running out of her. Sassafras had obviously been filling her in on Henemordonin's latest snatch-and-grab. In perfect Sydlynn Hayle form, she relaxed, one hip jutting out, a snort escaping her as her lips twitched in amusement. "Heard you needed help or something."

I rolled my eyes, shrugging. "Had it handled, as usual."

"Figured," she said.

We grinned at each other like a couple of crazy people, like this whole thing was actually funny or something. And, for that instant, it really was. We were the Hayle sisters, damn it.

A low groan broke our moment of fun. I spun to see Ram sinking to the floor, supported by Bakari's gentle guidance. My feet couldn't move fast enough, and I was certain Mabel wouldn't let me go, her hands hesitating on their grip until the last moment. As it was, I stumbled to my knees at Ram's side as his head settled into his father's lap.

"You have to hunt him down," Ram whispered, fingers reaching for mine. I leaned over him, focused on only him. He had regained a little of his color, but was still so thin and wasted I almost cried, my emotions in a turmoil. "Xeoniteridone hides on different planes, but I can tell you which ones."

Nice to know I was right. "Theridialis," I said. "Do you know where he is?"

Ram nodded, coughed softly, but didn't get to answer, not when the soft patter of feet forewarned Raethnn's arrival. She crouched beside him, as limber as I was, eyes intent.

"Where is Xeoniteridone?" Her hands grasped Ram's face, turned it toward her, her fury burning like a brand, so hot I feared she'd hurt him.

I pulled her grip from him, pushing her away, temper rising yet again. "Leave him alone. He's been through more than any of us."

She snarled at me like a wild animal. "My own people fall like late crops before the farmer to the Planeless. Our number, already small, dwindles to only a few." She shook, hands twitching, thick nails clacking together as they did. "And Demonicon will soon be no more." A thin wail entered her voice, though she shook her head and ground her teeth against it.

"Nothing we have done has had any impact. Only killing that *creature*," she spit out the word, power rippling around her, "will end this once and for all."

"Considering you had a chance to do so long before I met him," I snapped, my fury matching hers as I let my true feelings out, "I have little sympathy for you or the

Daeva."

She stared at me, white faced, and I was certain at any second she would strike, either with her hand or her power. But her icy fury died, the flames in her eyes flickering out as she accepted the truth of my words. "We have one choice left," I said, controlling my anger in the face of her failing rage. "Finding an antidote to free the demons from Xeoniteridone's hold and cut his power out from under him so we *can* kill him."

Raethnn shuddered past the last of her anger. "Impossible," she snapped. "No cure exists."

"It does," Ram whispered. "Theridialis."

The Daeva leader stilled, jaw unclenching. "You swear this is true?"

Ram sighed, eyes closing, the last of his energy gone. Raethnn reached for him, her power ready to wake him, careless, heartless. I blocked her, grasping her wrist so tightly my fingernails met around her slim bones. Her skin burned hot, firm under my hand, not the flesh of an old demon, at least not what I was expecting.

"The cure is the key," I said, holding her at bay while she glared her anger at me, but didn't fight for freedom. "Agreed?"

She nodded quickly, finally jerking her arm free from my grip. "Very well," she said, voice level as though she hadn't just shown such anger. "But when the time comes, we will kill Xeoniteridone and he will suffer greatly before he dies."

"Leader." Zinnia's soft voice brought me around. I didn't even know she'd joined us, hadn't seen her arrive and wondered at the safety of my friends back at the Seat. Did they take my advice and flee? I was sure Mabel and Zinnia would never let them come to harm, nor would Sassafras leave his siblings to the not-so-tender mercies of my black-hearted grandfather. "My nephew must rest, regain his strength. He will give us the information we need. But for now, we must no longer hold back anything from our Ruler." Her eyes met mine. "She must know everything if we are to be triumphant."

More secrets? That was almost enough to make me blow my temper to the stars and back. And from the scowl on Syd's face, I wasn't the only one who was tired of the demon penchant for hiding what was important until it was too late.

Raethnn's face collapsed and, for the first time, I saw all of her years piled on top of her, stretching back into history. She looked old and weak, reduced to a thin and trembling demon covered in wrinkles, her amber eyes sunken into her face, white hair thinning at the hairline.

"How can we, after all these centuries, have failed at our task?" Tears glistened, made their way through the crevasses and gullies of her lines, stopping to pool in shimmering drops at the point of her chin. She hesitated another moment before rising wearily to her feet, swiping at the moisture with shaking hands. "You would know everything, Ruler Senne Hathenemeira? You would see what the Daeva have kept secret since Demonicon was created? Then come." She turned and shuffled away, toward the door at the back of the room, while her two counterparts remained in their seats, heads down, faces sorrowful.

I stood and watched Bakari lift Ram into his arms, leaving through another doorway, hopefully toward rest and treatment and not more interrogations. Zinnia held out her hand to Syd and me, gesturing for us to follow Raethnn. I would rather have gone with Ram, but I knew whatever lay behind that door was more important here and now.

With Mabel hovering behind me and Syd at my side, our faithful Sassafras in her arms and Max following close, I joined Zinnia through the doorway, hoping whatever I learned here could help me defeat Xeoniteridone but not holding my breath.

I knew better than to get my hopes up.

CHAPTER EIGHT

A narrow corridor led us deeper into the Daeva complex. The black stone was so familiar, I almost felt like we were under the Seat. I was still pondering the location of the secret base, knowing now it had to be on one of three major planes still remaining to the Node, when Raethnn stopped and turned toward a huge door, the top of it arching overhead. It was the most extravagant door I'd seen down here, accustomed to the austerity they'd exposed me to so far. I followed the old leader through without a word, wondering at the tingle of power as I stepped over the threshold, hearing Syd gasp beside me while Sassafras let out a hiss of surprise.

The chamber was massive, the ceiling high above us cloaked in darkness, the floor as polished and perfect as that of my throne room. I did my best not to think about the fact it wasn't my throne room any longer while Ahbi shifted inside me.

Interesting, she sent. *There is a great deal of power here, but it's mostly dormant.*

I shrugged to myself and crossed my arms over my chest, coming to a halt as Raethnn stopped in the center of the room and spun to face us. Syd set Sassafras on the floor where he twitched his puffy tail around himself and watched with half-lidded eyes. I felt the presence of Mabel looming behind me, but instead of wanting her to step back, I welcomed her. She made me feel safe, not oppressed.

Raethnn raised her arms over her head, showing a surprising amount of muscle as her robe fell back from her chiseled skin, the withered look of her gone, her old confidence returned, to a point. She might look ancient, but time had done nothing to weaken her.

Jealous, Ahbi whispered. *I could have only been so lucky.*

I didn't comment, remembering the tall, muscular demon who held the throne before Dad and me, simply shaking my head at her.

"Behold," Raethnn said, "the archive of Demonicon." With that, she clapped her hands together.

And grew. And grew. Power poured into her, swirling up from the floor, sucking in from the walls, gushing down like a waterfall from the ceiling. Raethnn rose in height, filled out in stature, altered. I watched the years fall from her until she was a giant, young demon, still herself, but infused with whatever magic there was in this room. I might not have been able to access my demon power, but it was clear, from the sudden ravenous need of my sorcery, it was huge to the point of being bottomless.

"Like the power of Demonicon," I whispered.

"Correct," Raethnn said in a kind voice, her amber eyes circles of glowing fire, her pupils drowned in flame. "There were two sources created, one for the Daeva," she gestured at herself in slow motion, giant form moving slowly, but fluidly. "And one for the Ruler of Demonicon." She raised her arms again, the air around her turning into a massive hologram, one I felt devour me as much as my sorcery wished to devour it. "Come with me and see what we once were."

I couldn't take in everything and wished I could. Images swirled around me, of demons, lesser demons not nearly as evolved as the ones I was familiar with, eking out an existence, fighting each other, their sorcery, the monster living inside, taking them over as they killed each other, devouring the flesh of their enemies, their hearts, even as they absorbed the fallen's power.

"Once, we were animals," Raethnn said, "uncivilized, uncontrolled. Left to evolution, we would have died out, killing each other for magic."

I don't believe it, Ahbi sent, a hint of anger in her voice. *We would have evolved eventually.*

"We would not," Raethnn answered her, showing us more images, of planes almost bereft of demons, bodies piled, armies decimated. "We were close to extinction, Ahbi Sanghamitra. And we would have become extinct, if it weren't for the drach."

Max appeared, Mabel, more of the dragon race, focused on one demon, a general of some kind, ruler of his own plane. I felt my drach friend shift behind me but focused on the story.

"They approached Zelmanharitopel and offered him assistance in return for his compliance." Raethnn gestured, showed the gigantic demon, harsh-faced, but oddly familiar, speaking with Max and Mabel. It didn't hit me until Raethnn spoke again why he seemed like someone I knew.

"Our ancestor," I said.

"Correct." Raethnn changed the images, to more fighting, but less killing as the drach joined Zelmanharitopel in the fighting. "He agreed to the terms of the first race."

Max's rumbling voice interrupted. "To no longer kill for power," he said, tone soft, but carrying easily. "We would make him ruler of all demons if he would save them."

I glanced at Syd, whose eyes were as wide as mine, I was sure.

"And he did." Raethnn's hands fell as the scene

shifted to the Seat, a raw mountain, forming into the very place I knew so well and the battered general's procession to the throne for the first time. "Zelmanharitopel united demonkind, using his sorcery, and that of the drach, to pull together the Node and make one plane out of many."

A second seat was erected but remained empty. "Zelmanharitopel ruled Demonicon, but not before the drach enacted the final price he was asked to pay in order to save their people."

"Loss of their sorcery," I said, while Syd nodded.

"Your brilliance is his brilliance," Raethnn said with a soft smile. "Zelmanharitopel understood the need to still the monster within, that in feeding their sorcery, demons would simply end up right back where they had started and that demons would kill themselves off within a generation."

Zelmanharitopel bowed to the drach in the hologram.

"They understood the only hope for demonkind was to allow them to develop past their violent natures. And, in order to do so, they needed trusted leaders to guide and protect them from their natural calling."

Again the image shifted, this time to the Second Seat and the huge drach sitting in it. I gasped at the sight of Mabel's familiar face while Raethnn went on.

"Mabel agreed, for a time, to mate with Zelmanharitopel in order to give the rulers of Demonicon the stability they needed to maintain control of demonkind." I turned and looked up at her, though she wouldn't meet my gaze, her diamond eyes locked on the image before us. "From her was born a single demon child, half drach, who became the next Ruler of Demonicon." It showed him, diamond eyed, though they glowed amber, at the head of an army, and in the First Seat. "It took great power and control to maintain order in those early centuries. It was Aristonticabel, the son of Mabel and Zelmanharitopel who solidified the newborn order of Daeva to watch over the necessary rules, to keep sorcery from rising in demon power and to maintain order at all costs."

The next image showed a mate of his own, children spawning, growing up, spreading far and wide. "He and his many mates had hundreds of offspring, spreading the blood of the drach among the royal class to reinforce the controls over sorcery." Time flashed forward through two more Rulers, until an old man sat on the throne, a young and eager Ahbi in Second Seat. "It was the hope of the drach demons would evolve past their need to trade power, but our natures were not to be suppressed."

How well I knew that. I shuddered as Ahbi took the throne, Henemordonin at her side. It was odd to see Dad as a young demon as time wound continually forward. "Haralthazar showed the most powerful manifestation of drach bloodlines of any demon we had ever seen. And though we should have supported and encouraged him, instead, we feared he would be our downfall." She grimaced. "Though we would like to believe otherwise, demons haven't evolved far past our old, monstrous way of being. The infusion of drach blood has helped support the laws keeping our people from turning back to our feral nature, but that's as far as we've come."

Syd's hand crept into mine as we watched further, Dad leaving and us, amazingly, arriving.

"When we discovered Haralthazar mated with a witch from another plane, our concern grew." I squeezed my sister's fingers in my own as we watched ourselves interact, the memories coming back sharp and fresh. "And when we met you two, we were even more worried."

"Why?" Syd's voice made me jump as she interrupted the smooth almost hypnotic tones of Raethnn's voice.

"In you," she said, "we saw the demons you were and the drach like we'd never experienced. True evolution for the first time, though with outside interference. We understood then you had, thanks to your witch blood, moved well past our demon natures and, were you allowed to rule, would one day either be the salvation we needed from the violence of our pasts, or bring us, as a race, to ruin. Evolution can bring great chance and be a positive force." She bowed her head to us. "But it can also mean a species has outlived its usefulness and nature's next act isn't improving on the race, but causing its extinction. Not right away, perhaps, but by tainting our blood with yours, by placing the power of our world in the hands of those who didn't think or act as full demons, we ran the risk of allowing our people a new hope at change or the loss of ourselves entirely."

I shook my head, denying what she said. "We're only two people," I said.

"And you held, at one time, all the magic of our plane in your possession," Raethnn said. "Do you really think your influence hasn't altered our kind forever?"

Since she put it that way. Ahbi's mention of how the Node had been changed thanks to her and Syd just added to Raethnn's point.

"I can't believe change is a bad thing," I said. Syd nodded next to me, face dark with anger.

"And yet, we have held to our ways, to protect our people, for centuries," Raethnn said. "Can you not see how we might be fearful?"

This time when the image changed, I bit my lower lip while Syd turned her head at the sight of my sister crouching over Ahbi's dying body. My grandmother didn't comment, though I could feel her sadness. "The loss of Ahbi Sanghamitra meant Haralthazar would ascend the throne." Raethnn showed Dad on the First Seat, looking harried and unhappy. "From the moment he took power, we knew he was the wrong choice." I hated to agree with them, but even my sister was nodding a little.

"So when Dad abdicated in favor of Meems," she said, "you freaked."

Raethnn began to shrink, the power retreating from her, returning to the room. She aged as she did, body compressing until she was the same demon woman I'd first met, though her eyes glowed with magic.

"At first," she said. "Until we felt the potential in Senne." Her brow furrowed, lips turning down as she came to me and took my hands in hers, freeing me from my sister. "Forgive us," she said. "We have been too long wrapped up in our own self-importance to understand you needed us as much as we needed you." Raethnn shook her head, stepping back. "By the time we realized you were exactly who we waited for, it was too late."

Syd shifted beside me, arms crossing over her chest. "So we're part drach," she said.

"One of the reasons," Max rumbled, "you were able to become maji."

That was news. Syd twitched, scowled at him. "You could have coughed up that little bit of sunshine at any point before now," she said.

"Irrelevant," he smiled at her. "Would it have mattered?"

"Does that mean Ameline was part drach, too?" Syd quivered, as though the idea hurt her.

Max shook his head. "She had different origins,

though equally as powerful, to grant her the ability to transform." He frowned at the floor.

"Which were?" Syd shifted forward onto the balls of her feet, ready for a fight, though who would win between her and Max, I had no idea.

"Unimportant now," Max said. "Ameline is dead."

My sister drew a breath to argue, but we didn't have time for ancient history right now. Maybe later.

I turned and looked up at Mabel, speaking before Syd could, partly out of the need to cut her off and partly out of awe. "You're my great grandmother," I said.

Mabel's lips twitched. "With a few more greats added to that," she said. "But yes. I am." Her diamond eyes glistened. "And I couldn't be prouder of you, my dear. Unlike the Daeva, I have no fear yours is the spirit we've been waiting for. The magic you hold, the heritage in your blood, added to mine, means demons can finally move past their restrictive nature. The very thing we had hoped to accomplish but weren't able to achieve ourselves."

Tears burned my eyes, my throat thickening.

Well now, Ahbi breathed. *How interesting.*

"This is the reason the maji fear you, Sydlynn," Max said. "And why your power is far greater than even their most talented. Because you are far more drach than you are of their ilk. And you have the potential to evolve past them now that you have gained your full power. No maji/drach mating was ever successful. But in becoming the first new maji in centuries, you have fulfilled the role to the point they cannot tolerate the thought of you."

"And why Meira was able to break from the hold of the nectar," Mabel said. "No ordinary demon would have had such ability. Your sorcery will rival any, including your sister's, once you learn to control it."

I shivered at the thought, meeting Syd's eyes again. I used to feel like I was the lesser sister. That I would never be able to live up to Syd's achievements. Now I knew I'd been crazy to think that way.

And I wasn't sure it made me feel better after all.

"I've asked this question before," I said, turning back to Mabel. "Now we know its origins, if the planes separate and the Node collapses, what happens?"

My drach friend shrugged, long hair rippling. "We don't know," she said. "Since combining the planes was the first and only time we did so, we have no idea what will happen if they fall apart."

"But we do know this," Max said. "If the demons now have access to their sorcery, it won't be long before they devolve and the destruction of your race is assured."

I lightly punched Mabel's shoulder. "I'm with Syd," I said. "You should have told us."

Mabel's face fell, a flicker of worry passing over her features. "There is more," she said, "that even the demon Daeva don't know."

Max shifted, but didn't try to stop her. Instead, he

74

spoke to her in their musical language. The sounds blended like an orchestra, a holy choir of angels, filling the room with light and joy. I bit my lower lip to keep from crying as Mabel stared at him, stone faced. When he was finished, she gestured, a rainbow of energy falling from her fingertips.

"We have done many things we are not proud of," she said. "But our blurred past should finally come into the light. Especially now, with these." She gestured at me, at Syd. "They, of all, must know of our indiscretions and the darkness of who we once were."

He sighed and nodded. "As you wish," he said.

Mabel took my hand in one of hers and Syd's in the other. "My children," she said. "Know this. The drach are the first race, but we were not always as you see us. There was a time when we were mere animals, ruled by base emotions, but equipped with the most powerful of magicks to make the worlds the Creator supplied us into our playthings."

"What magic?" I had a feeling I wasn't going to like the answer.

"The first magic," Mabel said. "Sorcery."

CHAPTER NINE

I almost swallowed my tongue I gasped so deeply, and yet I can't say I was really that surprised, not after all the information we were struggling to process, my sister and I.

"What?" Syd was the first to speak, and I was grateful, perfectly willing to let her take the lead. "You said *what?*"

"From sorcery, all magicks arose," Max said, soft, mournful. "That is why it is impossible for other magicks to defeat sorcery—they are sourced from the blackness that devours all."

"We evolved," Mabel said, "Max the first of us to understand right from wrong, to develop empathy and understanding. It was he who united and taught us to be worthy of the Creator's gift."

"And it was Mabel," Max said, "who first discovered sorcery didn't have to simply devour, but could trigger the elemental magicks you are so familiar with. We experimented further, with different races," he sounded embarrassed if that was possible for a drach, "and discovered though sorcery's potential existed in all things, the elemental magicks springing from it were far more attractive and positive. No longer did we need to devour, but we could, ourselves, create as I can only imagine our Creator intended all along."

I seriously thought my mind was going to explode as I fought to process all they were telling me. Raethnn had paled again, one hand pressed over her heart as she listened, eyes gaping wide.

"You're saying," Sassafras spoke, reminding me only then he was there, "all living things have sorcery."

"Potential," Mabel said. "It's what binds everything together, the fabric of the Universe, but in balance. Overuse of it can create chaos."

"Even normals." Sass's tail thrashed.

Mabel smiled down at him. "Yes, dear cat," she said. "Even normals." Her eyes met Syd's a moment. "Where do you think latents come from in your witching world?"

Latent powers? We always thought normals with buried magic were old witch stock, powerless descendants of forgotten families. We were wrong?

"We helped the demons when we saw where their sorcery was taking them," Mabel said. "And we acted against the orders of Fate."

Max's head bowed. "My choice," he said.

"Ours," Mabel said. "All of ours. But, in doing so, we created a division in the Universe."

My mouth would never close again. "You created the other Universe?"

"Yes," Max said. "Our desire to help almost destroyed everything."

"A guilt we have carried with us since," Mabel said. "And drives us to maintain order in this Universe."

"While other races choose to stand outside," Max said. His rumbling voice hadn't changed, but I knew he was angry with the maji for not helping Syd.

"And, by creating the other magicks," Max said, "we split Fate in two."

"That's why the maji are so pissed at you," Syd said with a shake of her ponytail as her jaw clenched and unclenched. "You altered the single line of destiny."

"While breaking them into two," Mabel said, diamond eyes bright. "The Dark and the Light."

"Never mind the maji benefited from the creation of the other magicks," Max said, the soft tone of bitterness in his voice coming through now I was used to the subtlety of the drach. "The Light maji most of all. Their Fate understands it, but they will never accept."

"They considered themselves the true maji and their Dark brethren some kind of aberration," Mabel said. "Though I still believe their division was Creator's intent all along. How could it not be? The very fact two sides exist in balance is the utmost in Creator's plan."

"In the end," Max said, "no matter the truth or Creator's intentions for us, it was we, the drach, who caused so much chaos."

"And we," Mabel said gently to him as she smiled, "who have always made it right again."

When her diamond eyes met mine, I understood she wasn't just talking about repairing the damage they'd done. She was talking about making Syd and me.

Raethnn and Bakari left us there as Syd and I made a little circle with Max and Mabel. Sassafras remained firmly rooted in the center, silent and watchful.

"I get, now, why the maji refused to help me," Syd said, a touch of awe in her voice despite the wrinkle in her brow. "It all makes sense." She punched Max's arm with half-hearted effort. "I'm so going to make you pay for not telling me."

Mabel's soft laughter was so rare I stared at her. "Her stubbornness," she said, "is legendary."

Max cracked his own smile before sighing, the gust of wind from his mouth strong enough to ruffle Sass's fur. "And why they refuse to assist in repairing the veil, despite the risk to all," he said. "They have always blamed us for meddling in affairs not our own, though Creator never once punished us for our actions." His shoulders rolled in a shrug. "We were born a curious people by design, and grew into our empathy and understanding."

"Something the maji have never accomplished," Mabel said. "Until you were made, Syd."

My sister seemed uncomfortable with Mabel's praise, body stiff and shoulders hunched. "So they aren't just pissed at me," she said. "They're holding a ginormous grudge against the drach." I watched anger pass like a lightning strike over her face. "Short-sighted, arrogant, passive-aggressive—"

I could tell she was about to start using more nasty words when Sassafras interrupted.

"Let them choose the past over the present," he said with a sniff and a toss of his head. "In the end, when we've succeeded, it will only prove to them we don't need them at all."

"Perhaps a more dangerous fact," Max said, diamond eyes meeting Mabel's.

"Agreed," she said. "If the maji realize they are, in fact, unnecessary, it could drive them to act against us out of pride and bitterness."

"They have never done so in the past," Max said.

"They have had no reason." Mabel's hand fell on my shoulder, gentle but steady. "We have never given them reason. Until now. By committing ourselves to the cause of my descendants and ensuring their rise to power, we may have triggered the confrontation we've always dreaded."

"Hang on a second," Syd said, looking back and forth between them. "Confrontation? Are you talking about a war between you and the maji?"

Max didn't respond while Sass's tail beat a fast and agitated tempo against the cold stone floor.

"There are no guarantees of anything," Mabel said at last, breaking the silence in the room threatening to swallow us all. "And the future is only for Fate to see." What had she seen? It was clear to me she'd said something to him or they wouldn't be worried about this in the first place.

"And Creator's dark brother?" I wound my fingers in the netting of my robe.

"The mirror of Creator," Mabel said, this time with excruciating sadness. "But without the empathy or capacity for love and joy."

Creator's complete opposite. That was just lovely. "Do we have to worry about him, too?"

"Unlikely at this juncture," Max said, "unless the veil falls. And then, I fear, there will be nothing anyone can do to stop the destruction of both Universes."

"They are not meant to intersect," Mabel said. "Ever."

"We need to pay Fate a visit." Syd's voice growled deep from inside her. "Now."

"And the Dark Fate as well," Sass said. "Get both sides of the story."

Syd snorted. "Like talking to them ever did any good." She let out a heavy gust of air and tossed her hands, letting them fall to slap against her sides. "Doesn't matter right now," she said. "We have other issues to deal with before we can switch focus."

I shuffled my feet, hands clenching. "We need to talk about what we're going to do when Demonicon falls," I said. All eyes focused on me, Sass letting out a soft hiss at my words. "We know now it's inevitable."

"Maybe we should let it fall," Mabel said.

I nodded to her while Syd looked sick, as if the idea of giving in made her nauseated. But Sassafras eased up, his amber eyes flickering with fire before the flames died and he spoke.

"Maybe we should," he said.

Meira and I have already made that choice, Ahbi sent, startling everyone, including myself. *We need the rest of you to back us up when it happens.*

"We've already been away from the fight in the veil for too long." Max turned his big head to focus on Syd. "And while I wish we could be here to support you, we must return and ensure the safety of our Universe."

Syd's irritation was a banner on her face. "You go," she said. "I'm staying with Meems."

I fixed Max with a steady gaze. "Can you do without her?"

He hesitated. That was all the answer I needed. I took

a step forward and wrapped my arms around my sister, hugging her close.

"You have to go," I whispered in her ear. "None of this will mean anything if the Universe falls apart."

"We need to encourage the last of the collapse of the Node," Mabel said, bringing me around. "Speeding the end could take pressure off of my brethren."

"Because the collapse is interfering." Syd nodded, slow and unhappy. "If Demonicon finally falls, the damage will end and we can hopefully make headway."

So that was that, then. Despite my earlier acceptance, it took me a moment to blink the tears from my eyes at the final decision to let Demonicon fall. I knew it was for the best, for the sake of the other planes tied into the veil. And that putting an end to my world possibly meant the salvation of so many others if doing so stopped the degradation of the veil.

And yet, that calm I felt when Ahbi and I first discovered it had left me, and my insides quivered with new fear. Only the steady hand of Mabel, once again on my shoulder, kept me from flying apart.

"Our only issue remaining," Max said, "is the sorcerous power of the demons on the shattered planes."

"How so?" Syd looked like she needed more worry as much as a kick in the teeth. While she never really looked old or anything, she carried a certain gravity with her in times like this that made her look ancient, not just twenty-six.

"Their cumulative power could still cause issues," Max said. "Especially if focused and controlled. The second part of this task is to find and kill Xeoniteridone." He made it sound so reasonable and casual, though it was murder he was planning.

"We know nothing of his future plans," Mabel said. "And until we do, there is no way of gauging what kind of impact his intentions will have."

No counting chickens, in other words. I had to agree with her.

"The final concern," Max said, "comes from our past."

"Wow," Syd said, almost smiling. "So forthcoming all of a sudden. I'm shocked."

He did smile this time, bowing his head to her. "I know now it was wrong to keep this from you," he said in a gentle tone, tough to do in his rumbling voice. "As you now know, when we first began to alter the magicks, the upheaval created the Dark Universe."

"Meaning?" Sassafras's intent gaze pinned Max, though it was Mabel who answered.

"It is possible," she said in her calm, deep voice, "the fall of Demonicon will stop the damage to the veil. But, it is also possible that fall will, instead, open a permanent doorway to the other Universe and allow Creator's dark brother through to ours."

chapter ten

I sat in the chair provided for me, looking out over the vast expanse of water on the other side of the Seat. I wasn't all that surprised to be brought here to the surface, to discover the Daeva had their secret hideout, not in a far-flung location, but in the very Seat of Ostrogotho itself. My earlier wondering was confirmed when I stepped into this room and saw the familiar waters of the Obomar Sea stretching out in the distance past the shielding glass.

Raethnn quickly told me, in our new light of full disclosure, their base of operations had always been here, on the far side of the mountain, nestled deep underground, their surface level overlooking the now quiet waters of the bordering ocean.

Raethnn wasn't a bit apologetic when she showed me the truth, though. In fact, she seemed almost smug about it, forcing me to focus on keeping Ahbi from attacking her personally. Raethnn had been through a lot, too, so I let her have her attempt at this final cleverness out of the goodness of my heart. And because I needed her for now.

Instead, I took the large chair they offered at the head of the table—Raethnn sat at the other, a sign, to me, of equality which I didn't fight—and stroked Sassafras's soft fur. He perched in my lap, not a purr emerging from him as he stared with obvious irritation around him. Syd sat to my right, Mabel standing behind me, insisting on the privilege. Max paced slowly behind my sister, hands clasped behind his back, head down and diamond eyes swirling. I could only guess he was in communication with his people. And since there was nothing I could do to help him, nor he me, I chose to ignore his private conversation in favor of figuring out our next course of action.

"We don't have much time," Syd said as the last of the Daeva sat, Zinnia and Bakari among them. "Max and I have a Universe to patch together." He had just fallen still, turning his head toward her to listen. "So if you could throw the plan you have in mind our way, we'll get out of your hair and let you get to it."

I loved my sister so much. The confidence and casualness in her voice, accompanied by the crisp order of one naturally inclined to lead, set the perfect tone for the conversation ahead of us. I waited, hands folded around

Sass, as Raethnn scowled lightly at Syd before nodding once.

"Very well," she said. "You've chosen, as you informed us, to encourage the fall of Demonicon." None of the Daeva seemed impressed with our decision, but since they'd brought this on themselves, as far as I was concerned, I didn't really care what they thought of our goals. "How do you propose to do so, Ruler?"

Ahbi wriggled inside me and I let her answer. *We go to the Node*, she sent. *And we finish what Xeoniteridone started.*

"How?" Raethnn's hands moved forward on the smooth table as she leaned ahead. "You are a fugitive, hunted by Henemordonin. A target for the Planeless." I'd forgotten about that, how easily they could find me, get to me. And yet, they hadn't done so. That made me more curious and privately confirmed my thought Xeoniteridone wasn't ready to come after me just yet.

"The Node knows us, regardless of what my grandfather wants," I said. "The key to this will be completing the separation as smoothly as possible."

Very true, Ahbi sent. *If we push too hard, the planes will be damaged by the parting, not preserved.* Since we'd already gone through a major earthquake at the loss of Ilogabon, it was likely we could do more damage than we tried to prevent if we moved too quickly.

"Perhaps it would be wiser to simply let Xeoniteridone complete the task for us." Bakari's words were clipped with anger, so it had to be costing him to speak.

He may be right, Ahbi sent, privately this time, though from the swivel of Sass's ears I knew he heard her, too. *If we go bumbling in there with no clue what he's doing, we might just make a bigger mess.*

"Can we afford to wait?" Raethnn turned to Max who lowered his big head a moment.

"We can," he said at last. "My people have managed to cut off the last of the demon planes from the veil, temporarily. The influence Xeoniteridone and his plan are having are now limited to a small corner. However," he raised one big hand, "there is no telling, when Demonicon falls, if the backlash of the final separation will cut through that protection or if the planes will simply part quietly."

I had to trust the cult leader's intent wasn't to destroy the Universe. "He has a plan," I said. "And has had one all along. While I despise him, Xeoniteridone has managed to keep things together to this point. With the drach protecting the rest of the veil, it might be wiser to allow this to run its full course." I nodded to Max. "While being prepared for it and ready to act against him once it's over."

"It still makes no sense," Syd said, sitting back, the sound of her foot thudding against the table a steady beat. "Why would he give up all that power? Why fragment

Demonicon?"

"He has to have a reason," Sass said.

"What if it's to create bases of attack on other planes?" I shivered at the thought. "Bands of sorcery-fed demons branching out to steal power from the veil and planes heavy in magic?"

Syd's lip lifted in an angry sneer. "Sounds like something Belaisle would come up with," she said. "But we know the Brotherhood aren't involved." Her arch-enemies, the sorcery league back home, were ambitious until she handed their leader, Liander Belaisle, his butt on a plate during the battle for the stronghold.

"Xeoniteridone did say his handler no longer controlled him," I said. "That has to mean Belaisle."

"Which means he could have been set in motion by the Brotherhood," Sass said, "but lost contact when Syd shut them down."

Syd's irritation turned to deeper worry. She would make a terrible poker player. "If Belaisle is still active... but he can't be." She thudded the underside of the table with her foot so hard it jumped. "There's no sign of him."

"Not on our plane." Sassafras sighed while I hugged him, though it made me a little sad to know he considered Wilding Springs home and not Demonicon. "We already know how slippery he is. But, it's irrelevant. If he did set up Xeoniteridone to act against the demon planes, it was a long time ago—well before you defeated him."

Which means, Ahbi sent, *it's possible you'll be dealing with pockets of these kinds of issues in the future.*

Syd threw me a "why me?" look that almost made me laugh.

"We have to assume Xeoniteridone is working solo on this," I said.

"He is."

I turned with a soft gasp to find the source of that familiar and beloved voice. Ram stood, wavering but present, at the doorway to the chamber. He moved forward in stiff steps, though when Max moved to assist him, Ram kindly waved him off.

Mabel pulled a chair from the corner and settled it next to me, on an angle between Syd and me. Ram sank slowly into it, his face pale and drawn, but his eyes clear. I watched his nectar hunger crawl over his face as his eyes locked on mine, felt a deep jab of sympathy, knowing exactly what he was going through.

"You are in no condition," Raethnn began, sympathy in her voice, but Ram stopped her with one raised hand. It shook, the whole of him trembled with the effort, but when he spoke again, his voice was steady and his tone firm.

"You don't know the half of what he has in mind," Ram said. "But I do."

We all stared at Ram who shuddered, hugging

himself, unable to speak further. I reached out to him, freed one of his hands and held it in mine. His eyes returned to meet my own, jaw unclenching when I opened my sorcery to him and supported him. It was an odd feeling, so used was I by now to using my darkness to devour, not offer aid. But when I did, his sorcery answered me and, together, we gave him the strength to draw a shaking breath and continue.

I'd never felt so connected to him, and was almost lost in the way he felt when he spoke, wishing he'd remained silent a few minutes longer so I could absorb more of him. This was the Ram I loved.

"Xeoniteridone is doing exactly as you already uncovered," Ram said, teeth chattering together a moment before he settled once more, my power lacing tightly to his. "He is reverting as many demons to sorcery as he can." His amber eyes flickered with pain. "I couldn't react to you when I was being dosed, but I heard everything you discussed."

I could only imagine the pain he felt, but no. I could do more than that. My sorcery opened to him completely and, I was certain had we been alone, he would have fallen into me. As it was, he showed me only a fraction of what he'd gone through. And, in turn, I let him see my own trauma.

It was enough for both of us, tiny smiles shared, my heart healing where once despair lived, fear he would never recover. He wasn't whole yet, but Ram was on his way back to me and I would do anything—anything—to make sure he completed his journey.

"Is he going to use them against other planes?" Sassafras's voice interrupted, and I almost snapped at him, but Ram squeezed my hand in comfort before answering.

"He doesn't intend to leave Demonicon in pieces," he said, voice stronger, carrying now. I felt his disgust and self-loathing, soothed him with kindness and mirrored understanding. He'd been through so much, but there was more to come.

"What do you mean?" Syd leaned forward, eyes intense.

"Once Demonicon has split," Ram said, "he plans to reassemble it, but in his own image." Ram shifted in his seat, the sense of his nausea reaching me, making my mouth fill with saliva even as I eased his cramping stomach. "He's going to draw on all the power of his demon army to do it, feeding it from the veil itself." Max's brow pulled down, the sound of Mabel's growling upset washing over me. "The grand plan includes building a new Node, one that feeds on power instead of drawing on the delicate balance for stability. In doing so, he intends to make Demonicon the center of our Universe."

"The fool," Sassafras whispered.

"Indeed," Max said with more anger in his voice than

I'd ever heard from him. "He will destroy us all."

"The veil's power balance is even more delicate than that holding the Node together," Mabel said. "It acts like a closed circuit, circulating power through the system, keeping everything in harmony."

"That's why the veil is in such danger at the moment," Syd said. "The disruptions to the circuit are making it impossible to mend the holes."

"If we were able to put an end to the continuing damage, we would have a chance," Max said. "But if Xeoniteridone intends to continue pulling power from the veil, the wall between Universes will fall and there will be nothing we can do about it."

"And if that happens?" I didn't want to know, but I had to ask the question.

Max shifted his large body, diamond eyes flashing rainbow light. "If that happens, we can only expect two outcomes. One, a battle between the Light and the Dark with one winner."

"Or?" Horror gripped me though Mabel had warned of the 'or' earlier, fear washing through Ram and into me as mine passed to him.

"Or," Mabel said, "the contact will destroy both Universes instantly."

"Makes sense," Sassafras said, sounding much more reasonable than I thought anyone should at that moment with the end of everything looming. "A gateway is bad enough. But instantaneous contact between the alternate Universes would likely cause catastrophic failure of both."

"Agreed," Max said, the soft touch of sadness in his voice more painful than I expected.

Syd chewed her bottom lip, fingers tapping a rhythm on the table. "A new Node," she said. "There have been two so far, right?"

"Correct." Raethnn seemed relieved to change the subject. "The one now deteriorating around us is the second."

And the Dead Stone is the first. Ahbi's focus shifted to Syd. *What are you thinking?*

"Tell me about the initial attempt to create the Node." She turned to face Max.

He was nodding slowly. "Very perceptive, Syd. It was our thought the Node could be fed directly from the veil. But when we realized what was happening, that the Node was causing damage, we ended the experiment. It was Mabel who suggested making it a closed system, much like the veil itself."

"It seemed a logical solution," she said with great modesty.

"So you shut it down," Syd said, sitting back with disappointment on her face. "It didn't shut down on its own."

"I know where your thoughts are leading you," Max said, "but, unfortunately, no. It required our attention to close down the Node. And it fought us." He shook his head. "It took on a life of its own and didn't want to die."

Much like the Node we know, Ahbi sent. *It had a personality.*

"So why isn't it fighting Xeonteridone?" I sighed in frustration. "It should be fighting him."

Except, to it, nothing is wrong, Abhi sent, sadness heavy and cold in her connection to me. *He's been very careful to only take bits and pieces, instead of attacking it directly.*

"Tricking it into thinking it's whole," Sassafras said. "Can we convince it otherwise?"

I attempted to, Ahbi sent. *It wouldn't hear me.*

"And considering our plan is to let it go," I said, trying to soothe her guilt, "keeping it together at this point isn't going to work."

Ram's hand tightened on mine. "You're going to let Demonicon fall?" There was no judgment in his question, but I knew instantly through his touch his fear was as real as the rest of ours.

"Now that we know Xeoniteridone's plans," Raethnn said, "does it make sense to go through with the end of our world?"

"Do we have a choice?" I sought for an answer in Ram's eyes, but he shook his head, hanging it as he answered me.

"I know no way to counter him," Ram said. "Xeoniteridone's ability to access the Node comes from power I can't access."

I spun on Mabel. "Could he be one of us?"

"Us?" Ram perked a little. "Us who?"

The drach's unhappy nod answered me. "It is possible," she said, "he carries my bloodline much as you do. Tied to his powerful sorcery and his control of his demon magic, it is likely he's using all three magicks to do the deed." She looked away from me, to Max. "Forgive me," she said. "My need to protect them may have created their downfall."

I shook my head, mind whirling suddenly. "Don't go beating yourself up yet," I said. "If he can do it…"

Syd leaned forward and grabbed my free hand. "Then we can do it?"

"We just need to work out the logistics." I refocused on Ram. "And you're going to help us figure it out."

"In time to save the Node?" Ram's eyes were wide. "I don't think we can, Meira."

"No," I said, "not to save it. But to rebuild it ourselves, to counter Xeoniteridone before he gets a chance. And, if we're too late at that, to disassemble the Node he tries to create." Long shots, all, but these ideas were new hopes I never dreamed of having.

"Surely, when he sees the damage he's doing, he'll stop." Raethnn's desperation hid behind a thin veneer of calm.

"He won't, Mistress," Ram said. "He's completely

mad. The Universe could fall apart around him and he would laugh at its destruction."

Well, that was a lovely insight.

"We must find him and stop him," Raethnn said.

"Pardon the response," Sassafras said at his most droll, "but duh." His tail thrashed once. "What do you think we've all been doing? Twiddling our thumbs?"

I freed myself from Syd and stroked his bristling fur. "Nothing we've tried has worked," I said, a plan forming in my mind. One I knew no one would agree with and wasn't even sure was viable. "Hunting him does nothing."

"Then what do we do?" Raethnn's hands wrung before her, the gathered Daeva, Zinnia and Bakari included, looking so distressed I was amazed they actually had feelings after all.

"We set a trap," I said.

"With what bait?" Syd's furrowed forehead told me she already guessed my plan.

"Me," I said.

CHAPTER ELEVEN

The wave of expected protest lasted about a minute. I let them rant and rave, arguing with each other over the suggestion, while Ram's worry reached me through our combined sorcery and Ahbi hugged me tight.

It's an excellent idea, she sent. *But.*

But, I sent. *Only if he still wants me. And we have no reason to believe he does.*

Your grandfather sits on the throne now, Ahbi sent. *The very purpose of taking you was to have a puppet on First Seat.*

And since Henemordonin is working with them, I sent, *it's possible Xeoniteridone will have no desire to capture me any longer.*

Except, Ram's voice broke through, gentle and steady despite his continued suffering, *he's afraid of you.* I raised one eyebrow at him as he went on. *Terrified, actually. And that makes him furious.*

The damage I'd done him when I fought him for

Bilhaeder must have left the impression I was hoping for. And added to my belief Xeoniteridone was holding back from coming after me until he felt he could win.

So you think it will work? Ahbi's question hung between the three of us.

I do, Ram sent. *But you're putting yourself at great risk, Meira, with no promise of success.* It was clear what he thought of my plan.

If we're going to track him down and stop him, I sent, *we need the means to do so. Unless you know where he is?*

Ram shook his head even as the debate raged around us. *That is the one flaw in your plan*, he sent. *Xeoniteridone moves constantly. From plane to plane. You'd never track him. And once he had you in custody, you'd be lost to us, the effort wasted.*

Unless we were able to find a way to track me. I finally let go of his hand, though my sorcery continued to support him. My back straightened as I prepared to call the meeting back to order.

Syd was staring at me with her familiar scowl. When I raised my hand, ready to call for quiet, she whistled sharply, catching everyone's attention.

"You can argue all you want," my sister said, a growl in her voice, "but you're dealing with Senne Hathenemeria, here. If she wants it, she's doing it, and you're not going to stop her."

They all stared at me while I touched her mind.

Thanks for the support, sis.

Are you freaking kidding me? Her mental voice practically spit fury mixed with worry. *I'm about ready to lock you up myself.* She paused, anger retreating into frustrated understanding. *If I hadn't been in your position a time or two myself, I just might. But I know better.* Her blue eyes lost their intensity. *But please tell me you know what the hell you're doing.*

Will you take 'sort of' as a viable answer? She bit down on her bottom lip, the storm back in her eyes as I stood, pulling my Ruler persona around me like a cloak, face stiff and cold.

"I am worthless to you as I am," I said. "I've lost my throne, my power, I'm a fugitive from demonkind." No one spoke in argument. "I can't even stop the Node from falling apart." I gestured to Ram. "But, I can still serve by luring in the very demon we need to destroy to ensure the safety not only of our people, but the entire Universe." Let them gripe further if they wanted. Syd was right. I'd made my decision.

"Say he does want you," Sassafras said with barely contained anger. "Say he takes the bait and kidnaps you again." I could see the shivers running over his body as his fur wavered. "There are no promises we will be able to track him through you. Which means you will be lost to us for no good reason."

A growl echoed hollow behind me. "I found her

once," Mabel said, surprising me. She had? "When they took her, I found her, but we were too late to free her. She'd freed herself." Was that pride in her tone? "I can find her anywhere, I swear it."

I turned to her. "Because of our bloodline?"

She nodded. "More than that," she said. "You are the strongest of my descendants."

An idea budded. "Does that mean you can find any of your blood?"

This time she shook her head. "Not as clearly."

"But if two of us were together?" If I could link my sorcery to Xeoniteridone...

Mabel's smile made me grin back at her. "If you could connect yourself to him, and he truly is of my bloodline, anything is possible." She nodded once, sharp and precise. "I will be able to find him, too." Her smile faltered. "In fact, I should have thought of that previously," she said.

"Enough of that," I said, patting her arm. "Nana."

She snorted a laugh. "Is that the best you can do?"

"Gram's taken," I said.

And so is Grandmother, Ahbi sent with crisp coolness.

"Mabel will do," the drach said.

"Okay," Syd interrupted our family moment, "so we have a plan. But we need to keep an eye on the Node, too."

"Why?" I spun on her, frowning. The Node was

falling apart and we had no control over the rate.

"Because, if we miss by even a little," Syd said, standing herself, arms crossed over her chest, "Xeoniteridone will start making the new Node." She glanced at Max. "And I'm guessing, the state the veil is in, it won't take much to cause pretty hefty damage?"

He nodded, big hands fisted at his sides. "You are correct," he said. "Once the Node is destroyed, there will be nothing to cut off from the veil. Nothing to aim our protections at."

"Ostrogotho," I said, knowing it was true, that the first plane was the core of the Node and would be the focus of Xeoniteridone's attempt to rebuild the Node. He'd wanted it not just for the throne, but for access to the power of the plane through the Seat. It made perfect sense to me.

"Indeed," Max said. "Perhaps you are correct. But there are too many planes to protect and if we miss even one… our numbers are spread so thin already, I fear even a tiny draw on the veil's power will create a cascade affect we will not be able to stop."

"So we need to know the exact moment the Node is about to fall," Syd said. "So we can be ready to act immediately."

"We can contact the monitors," I said.

"Or," Syd said, looking through me, "we can send someone in to watch from the inside."

Ahbi must have known where Syd's thoughts were going because, when I gasped, she just shrugged sadly.

Your clever sister is correct, Ahbi sent. *I've been part of the Node before. It will welcome me without question. And I can keep you apprised of its condition and will know when it's about to fall.*

Grandmother. I reached for her, hugged her power to me, her spirit. *It's too dangerous.*

Dangerous, my left foot, she sent. *All right, I don't have a left foot anymore. But it has to be done.*

"What happens to her when the Node collapses?" I wouldn't let Ahbi go into this if it meant her loss. I just wouldn't.

Mabel's hands tightened on my shoulders. "We don't know," she said.

More uncertainty. But as I tried to argue with her, as the others tried to argue with me for my role to play in this attempt to stop our enemy, I felt Ahbi's resolve stiffen.

Irrelevant, Ahbi sent, brusque and professional past the core of fear I felt in her. *It's the least I can do. Meira,* her mind turned inward to me. *I've lived a long and powerful life, the least of which was what came before I met you.* I wouldn't cry, not here and now, though I likely would later. *But I've outlived myself by years, my dear. And if I can make this final difference, I want you to let me go. For you and for Demonicon.*

I hesitated. *Grandmother*, I whispered to her. *What will I do without you?*

She laughed. *Oh, my dear girl*, she sent, *you will be incredible. The finest Ruler to ever guide Demonicon. And I have no doubt you will succeed in saving everyone from disaster.* I tried to protest, but Ahbi cut me off one last time. *Your sister is correct*, she said. *I may not be a Hayle, but like it or not, you have my blood, too. And once we make up our minds, there's nothing you can do to stop us.*

I exhaled a long, slow breath and nodded to Syd. "Let's do it," I said.

chapter twelve

I stood to leave, the Daeva clustering together to whisper their own plans that had nothing to do with me, now. I was leaving to put myself into the hands of the enemy in the hope Mabel really could find me once I was in Xeoniteridone's grasp.

Ram had other ideas than allowing me to just leave him without saying goodbye. And it was that very act I wanted to avoid. I wasn't sure I could bring myself to go, not like this, when we'd finally found each other again.

He pulled me aside, away from my sister and the drach, and they let him, obviously sensing what he had to say was personal and private. Even Ahbi retreated as Ram leaned on me for physical support, face inches from mine as his amber eyes filled with fire.

"I thought you'd hate me by now," he said, voice low, vibrating with emotion.

Oh, right, I suppose I should have been angry with him for all that. "Why?" I prodded him with one finger. "Because you lied to me, to Ahbi, all this time? Made us both believe you were faithful and loyal only to us?" As I spoke the words, meaning only to tease him with them, real anger appeared. So it turned out I hadn't gotten over it after all.

Ram's hands tightened on my shoulders. "I never meant to hurt you," he said. "I wanted so many times to tell you who I was." He shook his head slowly, wavering a little. I held him up with sorcery, anger fading. "It wasn't fair to you and I've long disagreed with my leader's old ways of thinking." He hugged me suddenly. "You, of all Rulers, I knew was the right one to reveal ourselves to. And I intended to do just that."

"But all this happened," I said, wanting to believe him.

"Exactly." He pushed me away with gentle hands. "Now you know why I resisted you for so long, Meira. Not because I didn't care. But because I wasn't able to give you what you needed without you knowing the truth about me."

My heart leaped a little, a tingle of flame traveling the length of me. This hope I would embrace with all of my soul. "Now I know," I said.

He smiled, a wavering thing, eyes bright. "You do," he said. "But I have terrible timing, don't I?"

I laughed, hugged him again, feeling how thin he'd become, but how feeding his magic with mine helped to flesh him out once more, as though the loss of physicality came from the decrease in power. "The worst," I said. "But I'll take it."

This time, when we parted, I paused as his lips descended and touched mine. Shivers, sparks and a roaring in my head from the heat of his touch ended in a deep and satisfied sigh when we parted.

"We'll talk about this more when I see you again." I touched his lips with my fingertips when he tried to argue. I knew he would do his best to talk me out of the plan to infiltrate the Planeless, to give up Ahbi to the Node, at this point. But I couldn't let him. And if I allowed him to speak, I worried I might cave and just stay here with him and let everything fall apart.

Then again, why shouldn't I? But gazing into his eyes, I knew I couldn't live with myself if I didn't give us every chance at happiness. And that included taking our world back and patching it together again.

I left him with his aunt as Zinnia appeared at his elbow, her gentle support guiding him back to a chair. It was so hard to turn my back to him, worse when Syd's sad gaze met mine as I returned to her and the drach.

"Well?" I rubbed my hands together, the skin suddenly cold and tight. "What are we waiting for?"

Mabel delivered the pair of us directly to the Node chamber, the cold air of the underground replaced by the soft heat of the teardrop-shaped energy field hanging over a bottomless pit. I almost wept at the sight of it, so small, no bigger now than a basketball, spinning softly on its axis. What once was a towering core of power winked and glittered in the giant emptiness of the stone room.

I was glad Syd and Max stayed behind, needing to do this alone. But not so alone, not with my two grandmothers there with me to keep me from turning into an emotional mess.

Ahbi's spirit hugged me, pulled me close. *I love you, child*, she sent. So much for her support in sustaining my calm. This time, I did weep, if only because she gave me a great gift I never expected from her. She'd never used those words before, more precious to me than any other because I knew she'd rarely spoken them.

I love you, too, Grandmother. I clung to her a moment more. *I will find a way to save you, I swear it. And I'll do everything I can to make this right.*

You will focus on saving our people. Her tone was no-nonsense. *And I will do my part for as long as I can.*

I felt her pull away, hung on one last moment, and sobbed when her spirit separated from me, still connected by a thin thread of amber fire. I closed the gap between me and the Node, reaching out on my tiptoes to touch the edge.

Ahbi wicked inside, the connection between us breaking like the snap of a rubber band, the coil of magic that held us together for so long slithering back to me. I immediately felt her absence, the cold and empty hole inside me where once she'd lived. My arms rose in gooseflesh I rubbed away, tears streaming down my face as my grandmother's mind touched mine.

I will watch, she sent, feeling different outside of me. *And I will not fail you.*

My fingers brushed the edge of the Node one last time, my sorcery begging to feed on its precious energy. I jerked away as the dark flames fought to rise and backed up in haste, running into Mabel.

"Get us out of here," I whispered through my choking tears. It was impossible to look at the Node any longer and I hung my head as the drach opened the veil and carried us away.

Mabel hovered with me in the veil, morphing into her drach form. I settled on her shoulders, the crawling hunger of my sorcery more powerful than I'd ever felt it.

Your grandmother's spirit held the darkness at bay, Mabel sent. *You must now learn to control it on your own.*

I don't know how. I clenched my teeth, hands firmly pressed to her warm neck. *Can you show me?*

I can, given time, she sent, great wings sweeping the silent air in the veil. *My magic is far different from yours, however. It will take more effort than we have to give right now to make a difference. Perhaps your sister or the Steam Union you've both spoken of might be of some assistance, if we could even find a moment to make that a priority. For now, you must do your best to control it and keep it from feeding on those around you.*

My breath panted from between my teeth as I stuffed the black flames down and crushed them by sheer will. The grumbling unhappiness of the tumbling dark told me my sorcery was far from tamed.

I need access to my demon magic, I sent.

That may also help, Mabel sent. *It might be the best case scenario at this point, since we are out of time.* She hesitated, wings spread, hovering in the silence of the veil. *Are you ready?*

Was I? There was no real way of knowing. But we couldn't stay here forever. *Ready*, I sent.

I'm here with you, Mabel sent as we plunged through the newly torn gap she made in the veil. *Always.*

She shrank as we fell, her human form gently pushing me away as we landed on the stone floor of the Daeva's meeting chamber. Syd had clearly been pacing a hole in the rock because she spun with a scowl and strode to my side. My sorcery whined, she smelled and tasted so delicious, the rippling power inside her a sumptuous buffet we could feed from.

She must have felt my distress because her sorcery met with mine. *Are you okay?*

I don't know, I sent. *I wasn't expecting this.*

She nodded. *I know*, she sent. *Bit of a shocker, right?*

That was a massive understatement. *How did you keep from eating everyone's magic when yours woke up?*

I was surrounded by sorcerers, she sent. *A little easier for me. And I had a crystal.*

And she was maji in development. *Right*, I sent. *For now, if you can just stop me from devouring all of them at once, I'll figure it out.*

Meems. She caught my arm, pulled me to her. *You don't have to do this.*

I do, I sent, gently freeing myself. *Ahbi gave up everything to make sure this will work. I'm not going to waste her sacrifice.*

Syd let me go as I crossed the floor on unsteady feet. The magic in the Seat, the entire mountain, pulsated with energy my sorcery longed to devour. I had no idea Ahbi's demon magic held me back so well, and I found myself staggering into the table and using it to hold me up as a wave of hunger so powerful I could barely stand it drove a stake into my stomach.

Ram was still there, his sorcery linking easily with mine. *I know*, he sent. *I feel it, too.*

Just having him there, his touch so familiar, made it suddenly easier to take. He fed me and I, in return, fed him. Not a perfect solution, but it kept the black flames from rising to embrace the magic I felt around me.

Meira. I jerked my head up, felt the touch of the

Node, the whisper of my grandmother's voice in my head. *It's lonely here.*

I reached for her, but pulled back before I could make a massive mistake, like letting my sorcery have access to the last of the power holding my world together. "Grandmother is safely in the Node," I said to a chorus of sighs.

It's so quiet, she sent. *So thin and empty feeling.*

"She says it's almost over." Not accurate exactly, but I didn't want them to sense her weakness and the loss of her as she faded into the Node's remains. We all had enough to worry about without them doubting she could fulfill her part of the plan.

I won't fail you. Those words, repeated, almost made me cry again.

I know, I sent.

I've felt several attempts to sever the last few planes, Ahbi sent. *I think me being here is interfering.*

That could be a problem. "Grandmother thinks her spirit is keeping Xeoniteridone from completing the separation."

"He'll figure out a way around it," Ram said. "This might be a good thing." He nodded to me. "We still need to find a way to make you bait and to position ourselves to capture him."

"Kill him, you mean." Raethnn's grim expression and curved claws told me she wanted to do it personally, probably with her bare hands.

"If anything happens to you." Syd's voice faltered and came to a halt before she drew a breath and went on. "Meems."

"Syd." I straightened, pushing free of the table while clinging to my connection to Ram for support. "It's the only way."

"I will protect her," Mabel said. "With my life."

I didn't like the sound of that, but it silenced Syd's argument, at least.

"Enough talking," I said, feeling a sudden restlessness, an urge to escape the underground and be free. "I'll alert Jabuticabron and Sequoia of the plan. They'll be ready when we need them."

"If we need them," Zinnia said, rising. "Hopefully, Xeoniteridone will try to take you immediately and we'll track him and kill him, putting an end to this in short order."

"But if we don't," I said, "you all will have to be prepared to seize control of the Node when he tries to build it again." I turned to Syd. "I know you and Max have given us way more of your time than you should have."

"No," Max said. "This is where we need to be and, I fear, where we should have been all along. Fighting the source, not the result."

I felt better knowing they would be there if I couldn't,

to stop Xeoniteridone if I failed.

You won't, Ram sent. I met his eyes, bent and kissed his cheek. His hand rose to stroke my face. *End this, Meira. End him.*

Nothing would make me happier. I spun away from him before more tears could lay me low, though I knew he felt my sudden surge of sadness. Mabel waited for me, hands clasped before her.

"Bilhaeder," Ram said, his voice louder, firmer than it had been. "Look first on Bilhaeder."

chapter thirteen

I didn't comment, though it pissed me off thinking Xeoniteridone was using one of my few remaining planes as a hideout after all. Instead, I looked up into Mabel's eyes. "It's time," I said. "Let's go bait an evil sorcerer."

The air parted beside her, the drach elongating her face and hands already as she leaped through the gap. I followed without looking back, throwing myself into the veil tear, landing firmly on her wide back. *I will drop you in a quiet location and hide myself. You must then surrender to Xeoniteridone and make him believe you wish to join his cause. Otherwise, he will simply dose you.*

Agreed, I sent. *That's a better plan than what I had in mind.* Which had been nothing much of anything, to be honest.

Mabel spun on her wingtip and dove for a second tear.

Be safe, my dear, Mabel sent. *I'll be waiting for you.*

We dove for the new gap, her wings folding inward as she spun sideways and slipped through the thin gap. I did my best to hold onto her without the anchoring power of my demon magic to hold me in place.

The moment we touched the veil edge to Nunaresh, I realized something was horribly wrong. Mabel let out a cry of pain as the tear split in two, vibrating, pulling us between the two gashes.

MEIRA! Ahbi's voice reached me, but barely, though I knew she was screaming. *STOP! The plane is separating!*

Too late, we fell between the gaps, Mabel spinning out of control as the Node shed another plane.

Mabel shuddered as a gaping black hole, darker than even the veil itself, loomed between the two pulsing gashes. I clung to her desperately while her mind reached for mine.

Hold on! She tried to right herself, but we fell, her wings almost crippled by the pressure. I felt it pushing on me, then, as though we climbed too far, too fast, though we dropped like a stone into the depths of the emptiness. *I can't hold us!*

What is it? I knew I was screaming as much as Ahbi had been, but I couldn't help myself.

The place between, Mabel's voice crackled, broke up, warbled as though influenced by the void. She flipped upside down, my hair whipping around me, legs convulsively clinging to her even as her power trapped me against her. She flapped hard, wings carrying her up, but barely. I felt her desperation, the loss of altitude in a place where none existed. Even her gray skin, just beneath me, faded around the edges to black, as though the void wanted to swallow her.

And then, it hit me. The void, this empty place... *Pure magic!* I sent the thought.

The void is sorcery itself, Mabel panted into my mind. *Meira, you must escape.*

How? I looked up above us at the faintly glowing light of the two gaping holes, both now closing slowly as the planes separated.

Mabel grunted, a massive sweep of her wings carrying us higher, but just by a few feet. *Know I adore you*, she sent, *and that you are the finest of my children. Be safe, Meira, and save us all.*

Before I could process why it sounded like she was saying goodbye, she heaved one last wing flap, arching her back in a whip-like movement. At the same moment, her power released me, motion launching me into the air. I screamed into the dark, even as her tail surged upward and caught me, more gently than a child's swing, and flung me toward the far gap in the veil.

I clawed the air around me, trying to stop myself, knowing two things: if I went through that gap, Mabel was lost to me. And if I went through that gap, I would plunge to my death on the other side.

But my attempt to stop my forward motion failed and, just as I passed over the lip of the gap, I looked down into the empty blackness in time to see the flash of her diamond eyes before Mabel fell into the nothingness and vanished from my sight.

I passed through the gap just before it snapped closed, headlong toward the ground. My only saving grace was my entry, much lower to the surface than I expected. I plunged maybe ten feet, hitting the dusty ground hard, a mouthful of gritty sand choking me as all the wind left my body, flung face-first into the hard-packed soil of the plane.

A groan escaped me, half grief at the loss of Mabel, half a physical protest at my landing. I tried to roll over, succeeded on my second try, spitting out sand as I coughed air into my lungs. My stomach heaved in protest, thin liquid and bile spilling from between my lips while I clutched my aching stomach and did my best to pull myself together.

Boots appeared in my view, many feet, robes sweeping the dusty ground around them. I looked up, still shaken and disoriented from my fall, mouth gaping as I fought for air and the ability to keep from throwing up the contents of my body.

The single sun in the sky above blocked his face as he crouched, but the moment he came to hover over me, his body shadowing the bright light, I knew I'd fallen into the exact hands I was hoping for.

"Well, well," Xeoniteridone said while his son, Elphremantic scowled beside him. "A gift from the sky."

I was in his clutches, this part of the plan fulfilled. But without Mabel, the rest of it was a shattered mess. I coughed again, trying to clear my throat as Xeoniteridone stood, white robe gleaming despite the dust on his followers. How vain of him to use magic to keep himself pristine. And how odd of me to think of it in such a dreadful moment.

"Bring her," he said. I was jerked to my feet, my bones groaning from the insult added to injury, though I didn't think anything was broken. "I don't know why you're here, Meira, unless it's to trap me." He laughed as he turned his back. "Which I wish you luck with, my dear." I wanted so badly to pull free of his minions and leap on him, tear his throat out with my teeth. "But whatever your desperate plan, you're far too late." Xeoniteridone stopped and spun with a grand gesture of his staff. "My plan is much closer to completion than you might think." He pointed to a transport, motioned for one of the demons on board to come to him. She did, and I recognized my cousin, Tanasharia, grinning at me like she was having the time of her life. Considering how much she hated me, had for years thanks to the fact Syd and I displaced her father from Second Seat and put a pretty solid end to her brother, I guess I couldn't blame her.

"Now, dear Meira," Xeoniteridone said, holding up a flask of dark purple nectar. "We went a little overboard with this last time. But I think you'll find our latest brewing to your liking."

I could have fought him. I probably should have, but the results would have been the same. And at least the last time he fed me nectar, I'd gone feral and done him damage. In fact, he still seemed to favor his left side, something that brought me great satisfaction.

Mabel's plan to trick him into believing I was on his side was gone with her. In the end, it was the scent and my traitor sorcery that did me in. I crumbled in the arms of his followers who held me tight and fell into the song of the purple fluid he poured down my willing throat.

There was no creature fed by nectar waiting for me this time, no rage, loss of self. I remained me, in more control than I'd ever felt, calm, almost cold. My sorcery curled around me as his people released me, not the flames I couldn't tame, but a cloak of dark fire that was mine and mine alone to command.

Xeoniteridone clapped his hands, face twisting into a wide smile. I observed him as though he didn't matter any longer and wondered where the feelings I had went. I was acutely aware of my old need to hurt him, to take his life and, for a moment, I considered fulfilling that need just to see if I could feel. But the impulse passed as he clasped my hands in his, our sorcery connecting.

He was weaker than I, it was simple enough to sense it, though I doubted he knew how much more power I had than he did. At least, from his excitement, he had no idea. Again, I wondered how much it would take to destroy him. A single push against his heart and it would all be over. But he detached from me before I could act and the urge died as my curiosity passed from him to silence.

"What have you done?" I tilted my head, the sharp edges of my vision taking in the sight of my grandfather. Henemordonin appeared furious, agitated, more out of control than I'd ever seen him. A tiny part of me found that amusing, though it didn't last past the cold control stilling my thoughts.

"You meddling pest," Xeoniterdione snapped, temper turning so quickly my mind said "sociopath" even as I wondered why I cared he was insane and psychotic. "I've made her perfect. At last."

Henemordonin bent toward me, amber eyes full of distaste and more than a little fear. "You gave her the nectar."

"She will be a goddess," Xeoniteridone clasped his hands before him. "Controlled by me, of course." He laughed, on the edge of an insane giggle. Was he losing it as his power grew? Or was he this crazy all along?

Not that it mattered to me even a little bit.

"And I," he went on, eyes burning with fanaticism, "will be her beloved acolyte. And my son," he gestured to Elphremantic—I hated him, didn't I? Or did I? No matter—who joined his father, a smirk on his handsome face. "My son will be her mate and together they will be the Rulers of the New Demonicon."

Henemordonin's red face turned a dark shake of crimson. "I am Ruler now," he said. "You promised me the throne if I helped you."

I laughed, not sure why I did, except the sound escaped me before I could stop it. Elphremantic chuckled while his father's eyes narrowed, a nasty smile lifting his lips.

"You were a means to an end, you ancient waste of demonness," Xeoniteridone's hiss of contempt sent Henemordonin back a step while the Planeless closed in around him. "Did you really think I'd let you keep the throne?"

"You thieving, lying, pathetic, little worm!" Henemordonin's voice rose in volume to the bellow that used to frighten me, but now just made me frown a little at the waste of effort.

They snarled at each other, back and forth, while Elphremantic watched with a twisted and irritated grin. I barely heard their words, instead lost in the cold, calculating darkness of my sorcery. It was hard not to wonder how I'd ever felt anything but contempt for either of them, how petty and small they were, so insignificant. In fact, they were so tiny compared to me, I began to explore what lived inside, finding a vast and expanding power swirling around me, waiting to be fed so it could grow and grow without limits.

How simple to tap into those around me. I tested it on the weakest first, feeling how easy it was to siphon away their magic. Mine seemed to increase exponentially with the addition of fresh energy. Just how far could I take it? Clinical and detached, I pulled in more, feeling the Planeless followers sag as I drained their sorcery of their small resources and moved on to bigger targets.

I would have continued if Elphremantic hadn't chosen to join me, leaving his father and my grandfather to bicker. His hand traveled down my back, slipping over my backside, the other sliding up my ribcage to cup my breast. His breath smelled sour, and as I turned my head to meet his eyes, I felt a surge of the old hate return. It didn't last, but it must have shown in my gaze, because he dropped both of his hands from my body.

His touch should have made me ill. Instead, I watched him squirm under my gaze and tasted the edges of his magic. Not insignificant. Delicious, really, the best part of him.

So easy to make it mine.

"Now that you're one of us," he whispered against my cheek, "I'll coerce you into loving me." The need to laugh arose again as my sorcery tasted him further. "And then you'll do whatever I want you to do." He licked his lips, the expression in his eyes disgusting. Or would have been if such things bothered me. I was too focused on the yummy goodness of his magic and my sorcery's consideration of what it would take to strip him completely.

Xeoniteridone finally ended the fight. "Enough!" He turned from my grandfather. "Your services will be rewarded, as I said. Just not as you expected." He hit Henemordonin with a slash of sorcery, sending the big demon stumbling back. "And you'll be grateful for it."

My grandfather looked like he planned to fight again, but bowed his head instead.

Xeoniteridone's smile returned as he focused on me. "Now," he said. "Shall we return you to your rightful place, my Ruler?" His cackling laugh made my nose tingle with an emotion that died as fast as the others. But as he turned me and began to lead me away, I caught the look in Henemordonin's eyes as they fixed on me. And wondered briefly at the fury and fear he focused in my direction, tied to a very old regret.

chapter fourteen

My arm ached from being held over my head, gripped tightly in Xeoniteridone's grasp.

"Behold!" His voice carried on a wave of magic over the roaring throng of demons. "Your Ruler is among us!"

Detachment made it difficult to process the dimness I felt from the crowd, the quiet of their minds, though their voices were loud and growing louder by the moment as they celebrated my arrival. How odd, their false passion, controlled by nectar and their sorcery through the Planeless leader's grasp on them, as tight a hold as he had on me.

The last day had been a whirlwind tour of all the planes, carried down the devouring black tunnels of sorcery travel, myself pinned to Xeoniteridone's side, a proudly displayed trophy. I took the time to observe, held myself still and quiet, though I knew I could destroy him at any moment I chose. A small part of me knew I should feel excitement at the fact, but I couldn't muster emotion, not yet. If ever again.

It was interesting to see each of the planes on their own, one sun, sometimes two, a pair or handful of moons, the ground arid in places, deep, damp jungle in others, savannah and river and ocean and waterfalls of frothing pink all broken apart. Surviving without the Node connection which had held them together for so many centuries. Curiosity was the only thing I felt, though even it was dulled by the perfect calm of my sorcery and the nectar feeding it.

The zombie-like followers of the way of the Planeless fell silent when Xeoniteridone gestured for them to do so. Like a tap of water turned off, they stopped cheering, arms falling to their sides, eyes glazed and staring. The sudden silence raised goosebumps on my skin and I looked down at them with a stirring of that same curiosity.

When I looked up again, it was easy to spot the few demons Xeoniteridone had left whole, still in control of their demon power. Like evil shepherds, guiding the empty masses, watching over their silent flock. That truth cut through my apathy more than anything, stirring a faint surge of fear that quickly died. But not before my mind wondered if my people would ever be the same again. What if what Xeoniteridone did to them—and to me—

was permanent?

This latest assembly ended with a speech, one I'd heard so many times already I could have delivered it myself.

"My children," Xeoniteridone said with perfect tone and timbre, polished as the black rock of the Seat and shining like a new star in his white perfection. "Our time has come at last. We have shaken off the oppression of those who would make us in their image," an ironic statement if ever there was one, "and can now move forward into our true future. Are you ready to follow me to the path of righteousness and hope?"

They cheered again, this time prodded by their handlers. But the sound echoed hollowly to me, knowing, as I did now, their emotions were as dulled as mine, though I knew it was my sorcery allowing me to keep some cold awareness. Truly fascinating, if I cared for such things.

Xeoniteridone let my arm drop and gestured with his white staff. The stone at the summit shone bright, casting eerie light over the first three or four rows of demons crowded against the front of the podium.

"Prepare yourselves!" Nectar circulated like magic through the demons, their hands reaching automatically for the glass bottles, lips parting, throats swallowing before they passed it on with mechanical precision to the next demon in their perfectly formed rows. "The time is nigh."

One last cheer followed as Xeoniteridone turned and motioned to the air behind us. I caught Elphremantic's eager eyes as I turned to face the large, gaping hole, as black as the void, and followed his father into the tunnel of darkness.

Devouring black ate at my soul, nibbled on the edges of my control. Flashes of Mabel falling and falling twinged my heart and, when we emerged in wide concourse on the other side, I felt something trickle down my cheek. My fingers lifted, brushed at the single tear. I stared at the sparkling jewel of moisture, lifting my eyes from it to Xeoniteridone whose face had shifted from his standard geniality and softness to a frown of concern.

"More nectar." He snapped his fingers, suddenly impatient. I looked over his shoulder, all interest in the tear I shed lost, eyes traveling over the shining glass towers of the city we'd landed in.

"Nunaresh." My voice sounded harsh to me, long unused and sandpapery.

Elphremantic hurried forward with a glass bottle, the dark purple liquid inside sparkling with a life of its own. He handed it to me and I took it without thinking while Xeoniteridone spoke, the smooth, fiery flavor flowing down my parched throat.

"Very good, Meira," Xeoniteridone said, relaxing as I handed the bottle back to his son. The rush of power from the nectar solidified my emotionlessness, further pushing down any feeling aside from that ever-present whisper of curiosity. "Our home base, as it has always been."

"Perfect choice," I said, following him across the park-like central area to a floating bridge. I leaned over the side and looked down the long tunnel to the ground, crisscrossing bridges and floating transports hovering at multi levels in the upright city spires. "Planeless." I met Xeoniteridone's eyes, faint understanding dawning. The free city was the only one not to follow the plane ranking of the rest of Demonicon. "Is that where the name came from?"

He laughed, eyes sparking with flame. "Also very good," he said, though there was an edge to his voice. "You are far too clever, my dear. Always have been."

I didn't know what he meant, so I chose to ignore his words. They didn't matter to me, not with the heat of the new nectar making everything so clear and, oddly, cold.

...*fight*...

Someone whispered in my ear. I turned my head slowly, feeling my brows pull together while Xeoniteridone addressed his son.

"Make sure her doses are on time and that she's drinking," he said. "We don't want any slip ups."

"I can handle her." Elphremantic's arrogance used to bother me, make my stomach crawl thinking I'd ever believed he cared about me. But now, he was just pathetic.

"See that you do," his father snapped.

...fight it, Meira...

There was no one next to me. How odd. Where was the voice coming from?

"She's the key to the success of this," Xeoniteridone went on as the bridge came to a gentle halt on the other side of the central gap overlooking the city. I followed again without question as he and his son left the bridge and walked on, a small group of their faithful herding me from behind. "We can't afford to have her escape like last time."

"The new nectar is doing its job," Elph said in a bored tone. "Really, Father. You worry too much."

Xeoniteridone stopped and slapped his son across the face. I tilted my head to the side, processing this development. Elphremantic squealed like his father had delivered a death blow while Xeoniteridone hovered over him, face dark red with rage.

"You don't worry enough!" He stepped back, still angry but cooling down. I registered his instability with the same mild curiosity.

...Meira...

I had to shake off the whispering. It was driving me to distraction.

"You hit me!" Elphremantic's statement almost made

me smile. How obvious. And childish.

Xeoniteridone brought the butt of his staff down on the ground hard. "I will strike you again," he snarled, "and again," he leaned in to his son who shrank back, "and again until you treat this with the respect it requires. Do you understand me?"

Elphremantic nodded quickly, hand still on his offended cheek. "Yes, Father," he said.

Xeoniteridone turned his back on his son and strode away, talking back over his shoulder. "Get her settled," he said as he ascended a set of white stone stairs and swept past the bowing followers who lined the steps. "And watch her carefully."

Elphremantic's fear of his father morphed instantly the moment Xeoniteridone was out of sight. His lean face twisted into anger and disdain.

"Yes, Father." He spoke the exact same words as a moment before, but the meaning of them was far different this time, more sing-song, less agreeable. For the first time, I struggled against my lack of emotion in an attempt to understand the nuance.

...that's it, fight...

My moment of rebellion died as Elphremantic took my arm in a rough grip and began to drag me forward. My long legs caught up quickly, until I was almost pulling him instead. He snarled at me, tightening his hold until the pain turned to tingling and numbness.

The large foyer inside the grand house we entered sent our footsteps back to us in hollow thuds as Elph forced me toward the staircase leading to the second and third floor. I looked around while we ascended to the top, down over the white marble-like floor, the glittering chandelier hanging from the ceiling, the obvious richness of the place. It had Xeoniteridone written all over it.

Elphremantic relented his fast pace—if not his iron-like grip—when we reached the top of the stairs. He stopped me at a door partway down the hall and gestured impatiently at the cult follower who finally bowed and rushed forward to open it for him.

I joined him inside, taking in the expensive-looking and elaborate furniture, the huge, four-poster bed with heavy canopy and the lack of windows anywhere.

Elphremantic finally released me, pushing against me a little, making me stumble my last step. I turned to face him, the sensation in my arm returning with uncomfortable jabs of pins and needles as he eyed me with a leer.

"I'll be back to see you later," he said, one cheek still red from his father's blow, a light of terrible intent in his eyes. He licked his lips slowly, gaze settling on my chest. "I expect you to be cleaned up and waiting for me."

He left with flourish, slamming the door behind him, leaving me alone.

…*nectar*…

I shook my head, drew a deep breath. The whispering was louder.

...don't take anymore...

Who was that? Irrelevant. I had my orders, though I wasn't intending to clean up for Elphremantic's sake.

The shower was a welcome change, the hot water sluicing away the filth of the last few days. Fresh clothing waited for me in a small wardrobe room off the bath, my favorite skin-tight suit—in white, of course, Xeoniteridone's favorite color—and a lush fur-lined robe laid out.

I did my own hair, tying it up in a handful of braids would around the back of my head. And thought of Pagomaris. A shiver ran through me, unbidden, uncontrollable.

...save you...

Save me? From what?

...coming, just hold on...

Coming here? Who?

It didn't matter. Or did it? I focused on the whispering voice a moment, trying to force more volume. Maybe if I could figure out who it was and what they wanted I could make them go away.

But, before I could spend more than a few seconds at it, the door to my room opened and two followers of Xeoniteridone stepped through.

"Come," the female said, her tone deferential, but her

intent for me to follow her clear. "Our dear master would see you now."

I rose instantly, though, again, not because I was ordered. My curiosity seemed stronger than ever, perhaps a cause of the whispering voice? Regardless, I felt compelled to obey and did so without a word.

She and her companion seemed satisfied with my lack of resistance and spun, leading me out into the hall. We backtracked to the staircase and descended to the first floor, crossing the giant foyer. I caught sight of my new shiny white boots. I found them fascinating, staring at them as I strode with my guides through the house.

We paused at a large door, almost as big as the one to my office, though a single where mine were doubled. The female knocked, her long braid swaying behind her and waited for an invitation.

"Come in," Xeoniteridone's voice carried through the door.

The female turned toward me. "He will see you now," she said and stepped aside.

My hand gripped the cold knob and turned, leaving the two guides behind as I entered Xeoniteridone's private sanctum, the voice still whispering in my head.

chapter fifteen

He stood by a large window, a drink in one hand, his ever-present white robe discarded over the chair next to him. I closed the door behind me and waited, observing the crisp whiteness of everything in the room, down to the spines of the books holding place on his shelves.

Xeoniteridone finally spun and smiled at me, a benevolent expression I'd grown accustomed to despite the truth hiding behind his face. "My dear," he said. "Come closer. I won't bite."

I had no fear of that, no fear at all, as I crossed the room and came to his side. My eyes drifted to the window, gaze looking out the glass over the lush garden on the other side. "Pretty," I said.

"It is, indeed," Xeoniteridone said, setting down his drink. "But it doesn't hold a flame to your perfection."

I turned to him, a tiny coil of revulsion waking and

dying. "Thank you," I said.

Xeoniteridone patted my cheek, using the same hand he'd struck his son with. "Dear Meira," he said, sinking to the edge of his desk, hands falling to the thighs of his white pants. "You have no idea how long I've waited for this moment."

I supposed I didn't. "How long?"

He laughed, though my question was valid. I turned it over in my head, searching for the reason for his humor, when he spoke.

"I enjoy you so much this way," he said. "Though I wish very much I'd been able to allow you your natural state." Flames fired in his amber eyes, so pale they were almost transparent. "What a powerful statement we could have made. But, alas." His artful frown made me frown in response. "There was no way you would allow me the control I needed to complete my plan."

I nodded. "You're probably right," I said.

Xeoniteridone chuckled again. "Lovely girl," he said. "Just lovely." He gestured to a low sofa near the center of the room and I moved to it immediately and sat. The Planeless leader joined me, his glass in his hand again. He sipped, eyeing me over the rim, his power pressing against mine. I didn't resist him, curious at the action.

When he pulled away again, he was smiling. "It's true, then," he said with real delight. "Your conversion is flawless. I have to remember to thank that troublesome scientist. Despite his continuing rebellion, he succeeded in creating the right formula after all."

Scientist?

...Theridialis...

There was that voice again. And now I recalled, instantly and with perfect clarity.

"You took him," I said.

"I discovered he had an antidote for the nectar I used to convert my followers," Xeoniteridone said. "He couldn't be allowed to distribute it. But I knew no common formula would be enough to control you, not after your little escape the last time."

I felt my monster stir at the memory, before yawning and going back to sleep.

Xeoniteridone didn't seem to notice. "It's truly remarkable," he said, patting my hand with his free one, happy smile in his eyes. "And exactly what I need to make this plan work at last."

I nodded. "Sounds good," I said, not knowing what else to say.

Xeoniteridone squeezed my hand this time. "They had no idea what they were creating, you understand?" He shifted his body sideways, more to face me, expression lighting with delight tinted by old bitterness. "Nor that I would so quickly outgrow them. You and I, Meira, we are meant for bigger things than those who made us could ever know."

"Bigger things?" There was the curiosity again. But Xeoniteridone didn't seem to mind. In fact, he grew even more eager, leaning toward me, eyes glowing with fanatic excitement.

"Absolutely," he said, a fine spray of his spit touching my cheek as his enthusiasm grew. "They made me to use me. Just as your parents made you for their purpose."

I didn't think that was the case, but maybe he was right. After all, when I was born, Syd was already rejecting her magic. Did Mom and Dad have me just so Mom would have an heir? That backfired on her when I was born with demon coloring I was forced to hide my whole young life. A trace of his resentment rubbed off and I nodded to him to continue.

"The Brotherhood made you," I said.

"Those fools." He snorted, sipping his drink, expression darkening a moment. "They trapped a demon woman, forced her to breed with my sorcerer father. And I was the result."

Interesting.

...horrifying...

I ignored the whisper as he went on.

"They wanted to use me against your grandmother," he said. "A small and petty plan, one that fell apart when your darling sister and her enemy ended up killing Ahbi Sanghamitra."

Syd wasn't part of that. Ameline was the murderer.

But I didn't bring up the discrepancy, too fascinated by the churning emotions Xeoniteridone showed me as he continued his story.

"The Brotherhood's lack of foresight was my salvation," he said, tipping his glass to me with a wink. "When my father and his handlers finally ran from your sister, they left me with the means to do as I intended all along—follow my own path to my full potential and do what no other demon has ever done."

So the Brotherhood had everything—and nothing—to do with this.

...tell Syd...

The whispering confirmation somehow made me feel even calmer. I continued to observe as Xeoniteridone rose and refilled his glass from a crystal decanter, the sound of the top being replaced making my teeth oddly ache. He turned toward me so the rays of the sun coming through the window cast amber beams over the floor. Tiny dust motes floated in the beam, catching and holding my attention even as he spoke again.

"I created my own son," he said, though, from his tone of voice, his unhappiness with Elphremantic was stronger than his pride. "Chose to use my sorcery to free all demonkind and recreate our world."

"In your image," I said without thinking, triggered by the speech he made.

Xeoniteridone's scowl told me I'd said the wrong

thing. "Our sorcery was stolen from us," he hissed at me, "by the oppressors who created the Node and those meddling drach." The words spit from his lips. But he quickly recovered, straightening, returning to the couch beside me. "I choose full control of my power over the stunted growth we were offered as a race."

I wound those words around in my head a moment. Was it another line he fed me or did he really believe we deserved to be free?

"Sorcery is dangerous for us," I said, the words stumbling from my mouth as I frowned around the idea in my head, the calm trying to keep me from forming thought. "The monster within won't let us survive."

Xeoniteridone's eyes narrowed. "So you've been taught," he said.

Perhaps.

...you've felt it, Meira...

Yes, yes I had. Hadn't I?

Xeoniteridone leaned toward me again, taking my hand in his, voice soft and coercive as his sorcery wrapped around me, tasting my power. "Your grandfather understood," he said. "Henemordonin saw the way our people have been held to a lower standard, held back from our true potential. And his willingness to support me has made it easier for this plan to proceed. How magnificent you've been, Meira, fighting me. But now you know the truth, don't you?" His coercive magic leaned hard on me, shoving down even the curiosity, silencing the voice whispering in my mind.

I nodded, all forgotten, the dead calm and coldness embracing me.

"Of course," I said. "You need me. I'm the key." I paused. "Why?"

His power backed off though he remained in physical close proximity. I smelled the alcohol on his breath, not nectar as I'd thought but some kind of distilled beverage like whisky from home. "As soon as I saw you, I felt how powerful you truly were. When you and your sister first arrived on Demonicon, I saw your capacity for strength."

He saw me then? "Where were you?" My questioning survived his coercion after all.

What else had?

"I've been watching you a very long time," he said with a mysterious twinkle in his eyes, leaning back from me, a satisfied smile pulling on his lips. "Your sister might have had most of the attention, but it was you, I knew, who would serve me the best. And you have, my dear. You have. And you will even more so as I complete the dissolution of Demonicon and begin the rebuild with you at my side."

...can't let him...

Why not?

...ask him again why he wants you...

I found myself obeying the whisper as I would have

Xeoniteridone.

"You've given me to your son," I said. "But you want me for yourself."

The whisper hissed at me that wasn't what I was supposed to say, but Xeoniteridone nodded and I ignored the voice in my head.

"It is true," he said. "I would prefer to mate with you myself." I stared silently into his eyes. Should that statement have bothered me? Perhaps. "But if our plan is to work, if the final recreation of the demon race is to happen, I must fulfill a different role. That of your faithful and trusted church leader while you and my son sit on the thrones of Demonicon." Xeoniteridone sneered suddenly. "He doesn't deserve you, I admit. He has been a disappointment from the moment he was born." Xeoniteridone shook his head, white hair moving with his motion. "But he's all I have to work with and you, my dear, will be First Seat and, I hope, in time, will come to naturally accept our new roles to the point I won't have to use coercion against you." His eyes glittered with hope and a touch of melancholy. "I do so pray for the day you and I work as one, Meira."

...sick bastard...touch her and I'll kill you myself...

I knew that voice. It was coming back to me, as the volume rose and the woman's angry tone cut into the clarity I now knew was fog around my mind.

Xeoniteridone didn't notice, leaning away again with a

sigh.

"For now, my dear," he said, "you must fulfill your role under the controls of nectar and my power. Unfortunate, but true. Still, I'm confident you will come around when you see how much better things will be once I've created a new demon race from the ashes of the old."

...please, Meira, you have to listen...

I am, I sent, my power sullen as I felt the monster stir against Xeoniteridone's hold at last. *I'm here, Grandmother.*

Now, to find a way to stay present, even a little, without showing my hand.

Chapter Sixteen

A knock at the door disturbed Xeoniteridone's focus on me. When it opened before he could say enter, his deep scowl told me his son's entry wasn't welcome. But Elphremantic ignored his father's temper by holding up a glass bottle with the familiar nectar inside.

"It's time for her dose," he said as though trying to sound casual. But I saw the eager tension in him and wondered what it meant on the surface, while my insides crawled and yelled at me about as loudly as the voice now speaking at full volume.

Xeoniteridone waved vaguely in my direction. "I'm done with her for now, anyway. Take her and make sure she's secure before you dose her again. I don't want any mistakes this time."

"So you've said," Elphremantic said in just the right tone to keep his father from losing his temper. I knew that tone, hadn't mastered it myself.

The moment you get him alone, Ahbi sent to me, much clearer now I knew it was her, *you kill that nasty little bastard. You understand me, Meira?*

I understood well enough, but I couldn't bring myself to act. Instead, I rose as I was bid when Elphremantic gestured to me and left with him, pausing at the door when his father called after us.

"I'm counting on you, boy," he said with a measure of threat. "Don't disappoint me."

Elphremantic didn't comment, just closed the door behind me. The moment it was sealed, he snarled at the portal.

"We'll see, Father," he said before grasping my arm again, in the exact spot as before, triggering pain as the old bruising awoke. "Come on."

I kept pace with him easily, more and more of the real me rising as we strode to the stairs and began to climb. It was as though the physical exercise burned off more of the coercion and control of the nectar.

That and I'm pouring everything I have into you, Ahbi sent. *Do you have any idea how hard it was to find you?*

How? I wanted to shudder, to jerk myself free of Elphremantic, but my body was still under the control of the nectar, if not my mind. The fog creating the fake calm in me was burning off by the second.

I've had help, Ahbi sent. *Nunaresh might not be connected to the Node anymore, but it used to be. And I was part of it. It's taking a lot of effort to talk to you over the distance, but I couldn't leave you alone once I found you.* Her distress was as clear as her voice thought that seemed to be fading. *I'm running out of energy, Meira. You have to act against them.*

I know, I sent as Elphremantic spun me, not at the third floor as I expected, but on the second, turning me the opposite direction and down the hall, to where, I had no idea. Somewhere secure, his father said. A cell or a prison, perhaps? *I'll find a way. Grandmother.* I choked inwardly on tears thought my face remained stoic. *Mabel is gone.*

Her sadness touched me. *We know already*, she sent. *Max felt my warning and her fall into the void. They are trying to find her.*

The Node? I bumped into Elph as he came to an abrupt halt outside another door. He released me briefly to jerk it open, his other hand still occupied by the bottle of nectar, before placing his palm between my shoulder blades and propelling me into the room. I pulled myself to a halt only two steps inside, glancing at him as he closed and locked the door behind him.

Some secure area. This had to be his quarters, and being in them alone with him made bile rise in the back of my throat. He had to have more than just dosing me in mind if he brought me here.

We're still holding together, she sent, *but barely. That doesn't*

146

the nectar's dimming effect, the fog rising, forcing my emotions back. Again, my sorcery screamed her defiance, and I reached out to her, perhaps to silence her or to comfort her.

Not that it mattered. The second I touched her, really opened to her and let her out, she roared into life. In that moment, I found again the creature I had been, the new nectar waking the change in me, but under my control. With a roar, the ancient demon in me exploded outward, filling me with her rage and need to feed.

But this time, instead of taking over, my mind and consciousness solidified in the forefront. Emotions returned in a rush, and knew this was Theridialis's gift. Not the lack of effect, but the enhancement of it. How did he know I was able to take control of my sorcery? Perhaps a guess based on Syd, on my human parentage. Regardless, the nectar, instead of numbing me, now fed me as it raced through my veins. With the waking of my ancient demon form, Theridialis gave me the ability to burn away the false numbness he created as a mask for the true purpose of the nectar he made just for me, to help me evolve—or devolve?—into the form I needed to fight back.

I snapped into full awareness, sharp edged and clean, real instead of a fake fog created by Xeoniteridone and the nectar. This time I was the monster and she obeyed me.

Elph's mouth was locked in the space between my breasts, hands clumsily massaging them as he grunted into my cleavage. A single flick of power sent him flying backward with a cry of pain, to crash into the wall. I raised one hand, a coil of blackness pinning him, raising him above the floor by a hold around his neck. He clawed at the band of darkness, kicking his feet to no effect beneath him, face turning redder and redder as I approached in slow strides, barely holding back my fury.

He squeaked as I debated draining him.

No time, Ahbi sent while my monster snarled at her. *Can't you feel it?*

I did. The Planeless were coming, had sensed the change in me, through Xeoniteridone. Only then did I feel his sorcery linked onto mine, an early warning system I hadn't felt until now. And since Elphremantic was a minor irritant compared to the main target, I let him fall, though I hit him firmly one more time to knock him out first. My monster sampled his power, took some for herself, and I didn't begrudge her the taste.

But we had a larger meal ahead of us, one most satisfying.

The door was already opening when I turned toward it, letting my monster take over. My body swelled upward and outward, muscles bulging, my vision tightening and becoming hyper sensitive. One glance at my hands as I raised them to gesture and I knew I was now in the full throes of my sorcery's need.

Not that I cared, though the gnarled and claw-like giant mitts I now wielded made me wonder what the rest of me looked like. Irrelevant as I stomped my way, new boots shredded, most of my body-suit in fragments around me, through the guards. Bones crunched, screams echoed as my feet pulped legs and arms, power flinging the Planeless attacking me with the ease of a child's discarded toys.

If it hadn't been such a desperate situation, I would have said it was fun. Oh, who was I kidding? I laughed as I slid down the bannister and to the first floor like a giant ape with seemingly limitless agility and power, one arm extended, taking out a handful of guards who tried their best to bring sorcery and demon power against me. I caught a flicker of white and a shocked face from Xeoniteridone's office before he lunged out to attack me as well.

Perfect, exactly who I was after.

Meira. Ahbi's mind cut through. *Do you feel that?*

I wanted to tell her to shut up as I hit the bottom, my feet impacting so hard I felt the ground shake. But she prodded me with the touch of a familiar demon and I pulled up short, a shield of sorcery between me and Xeoniteridone. He slammed his power against me, his people doing the same—at least, those who still could and weren't crippled and moaning already.

Theridialis. I knew that mind anywhere, felt the tug through the nectar feeding me. So clever, that demon. He'd not only given me a back door to control my power, he embedded the sense of himself in it so when I drew close enough, I'd know he was nearby. *Where is he?*

Here, somewhere, Ahbi sent. *We need to find him.*

I hit Xeoniteridone, sent him skidding back across the floor. *I can kill him now,* I sent.

We need that antidote, too, Ahbi sent as a veritable horde of Planeless suddenly poured through the front door. *And you're sadly outnumbered.*

I can take them, I grumbled as my monster protested retreat.

We're not running, Ahbi sent. *But we need to rescue Theridialis. Now, Meira.*

I knew she was right. My narrow window of killing Xeoniteridone had closed. Sorcery bombarded me, tried to shut me down as the gathering Planeless poured everything they had at me, shielding their fleeing leader. The pressure of all that sorcery was more than even I in my present state could handle. I roared at them, shoved them all back with a massive effort and output of sorcery before jerking open a portal and diving into it.

Ahbi's voice was gone a moment, but my monster—and the creature I'd become—remained. I stopped inside the tunnel of black, surprised not to feel the ever-devouring presence, realizing then I was immune in my present state and making me wonder if the drach had done us a disservice after all. Was this, what I'd become, our natural evolution? Demons who could control the darkness within?

A topic of inquiry for another time. Right now, I had a scientist to rescue. I had doubts I'd be able to feel him from the dark place in which I now hid, but, to my shock, his energy came through loud and clear.

I pinpointed his location and opened the other end of the tunnel, diving out in attack mode, ready to take on the Planeless. Only to leap into a cramped and musty cell, to the sight of a much-reduced, but familiar form hovering in the corner, his hands bound by short chains to the wall, but his spirit unbroken.

"Whatever foul creature you've sent this time," he yelled into the air, "I will never cave to you, Xeoniteridone. I am a free demon and will remain so forever."

"Theridialis," I said, voice a growling roll of thunder. "It's all right. I'm here to take you home."

He spit in the filthy straw at his feet, trembling, large belly no longer in existence, face drawn and lined. "Evil one," he said. "I will not believe your lies."

"It's me," I said, not wanting to let go of my monster just yet and hoping he'd recognize me through the feel of my sorcery as I touched him with a tendril of energy. "Meira."

Theridialis stared a long moment before relaxing, jaw slack. "Meira," he whispered. "Can it be?"

"Your nectar did the job," I said, moving slowly toward him in case he freaked out on me again. But he just watched with intense fascination, his fear gone, as though forgetting where he was and what he'd been through. At a closer range I not only smelled him—Xeoniteridone hadn't allowed him to bathe, clearly—but I saw the dark bruising on his face and arms under the tint of his skin. "You made the perfect demon."

He smiled at me, clapping his hands together, making his cuffs jingle. "Meira," he said, bright and happy. "How delightful."

I couldn't help but laugh, a coughing snarl that came out all wrong. Theridialis didn't flinch, reaching out to touch me as I closed the last step and used sorcery on his cuffs.

"Well done, dear one," he said, sagging against me as his energy flagged. "I hoped it might trigger just the thing."

"I just wish I'd known sooner," I said, lifting him into my arms. Theridialis had been a large demon, but even his short stint in captivity had deflated him like a punctured balloon. He felt like a feather in my arms. "I would have saved you from all this."

"No matter," he whispered to me, head on my shoulder. "I have the antidote. And if you take me to my lab, I'll make it for you so this can all be over."

Hope leaped to life in my heart as he passed out against my chest. I turned from the wall, toward the bars, reaching for my sorcery, to the sound of pounding feet coming closer.

Stay and kill Xeoniteridone? Or save my people?

Either way, the Planeless leader was going to die. Responsible Ruler time.

I carried the unconscious scientist into the darkness just as the first of the Planeless appeared to try to stop me.

"Tell Xeoniteridone," I shot at them as I stepped through, my shielding holding off their feeble attempts, "I'll be right back."

chapter seventeen

I stepped out of the black and into the Daeva's main chamber overlooking the ocean, locked onto the feeling of my sister and the sorcery of the Daeva. It helped they hadn't left the last room I'd been in before my ill-fated flight with Mabel, making them easy to track and use as a beacon. All my concerns about my drach ancestor came flooding back as the occupants of the room reacted with varying degrees of upset at my sudden appearance.

Bakari's magic hit me the same moment Raethnn's did, though neither made it through my shields. I managed to block them both, but knew a pending double strike from Syd and Max would be my end if I didn't manage to convince them. I shouldn't have worried. My sister spun and threw energy at the Daeva instead, halting further attacks.

"It's Meira!" She turned back, blue eyes huge. "Isn't

it, Meems?"

"Syd." I offered Theridialis as she hesitated. "Help him, please. He has the cure."

She rushed forward, face distressed. "Theridialis." Sassafras's silver body streaked forward, leaping up to land on his father's chest. His amber eyes looked up and met mine. "Thank you," he whispered.

"My pleasure," I said.

"Nice muscles." He head-butted me. I glanced to my right at the smooth glass throwing back my reflection. It was only a hazy image, barely formed, but enough I got the gist of my new, hulking appearance. I'd give an Unseelie troll a run for her money. "We were worried about you. Because of last time."

"Turns out," I said, handing Theridialis off to Bakari who carried him brusquely away, Sassafras transferring himself briefly to my shoulder, "your father was far more clever than Xeoniteridone expected."

I felt my monster shudder and sigh, her power retreating slowly, grudgingly. Though I appreciated her presence not so long ago, it felt good to shrink, returning to my normal form, though, within moments, I was very embarrassed to be mostly exposed to the gathering. Zinnia hurried forward as Sassafras hopped down, slipping free her shawl and wrapping it around me before my embarrassment could kill me. I might have been a demon, but I was also raised by a witch, and modesty still burned my cheeks when I was caught outside my comfort zone.

Ram stared with burning eyes, making things all the worse, really. If only because I wished we had a moment or two to explore his feelings toward my half-nakedness. Which, I was sure would lead to full nakedness, and we just didn't have the time.

For now.

Good girl, Ahbi chuckled in my head. *Priorities.*

"I'm going back," I said, already reaching for the darkness inside me. Though weary, my monster was more than willing. "I know where Xeoniteridone is and I don't want to give him a chance to escape." Which he probably had already, but I was going to make sure of it, just in case. "Theridialis said he can make the cure, so get on that, why don't you?"

"Meems," Syd reached for me, her power stopping me, but gently. "You know he's probably already fled."

Why did she have to say it out loud?

She's right, you know, Ahbi sent. *Your place is here. More so, your place is on the Seat. We need to take it back.*

Syd was nodding, and I knew Ahbi included her in the conversation. "Let the antidote take away Xeoniteridone's power. Then we go after him, when he's reduced."

It did make sense. And this was the first hope we'd had in a long time, since this mess started, really. I shrugged and hugged myself, the thin shawl barely warming me. Now that I'd stopped running, fighting, the nectar burned out of my system, I felt tired to the bone.

"Mabel?" My head came up as I met Max's gaze. He didn't seem concerned, though he didn't answer right away.

"We looked for her." Syd glanced over her shoulder at him before hugging me gently. "We couldn't find her."

"The void between planes, between the veil's existence, is an empty place," Max said, soft, unjudging, though I was now judging myself with time and the mental capacity to think things over and lay blame. "But though she is lost within it, it should do her no lasting harm. We will locate her when this battle is over and we can assemble the full power of the drach race in search."

I tried to let his words make me feel better, but I still felt like I let her down. "I'll be coming with you," I said.

He nodded. "I knew you would have it no other way." Max turned his attention to my anxious sister. "We must return to the veil. The last of the planes could separate at any moment."

I knew what that meant. "Just in case everything falls apart," I said to my sister, hugging her myself this time. "I love you, Syd."

"Silly," she whispered in my ear, "I'll see you soon, okay?"

I nodded, throat tight, knowing we had no choice

regardless, whether the Universes were about to implode or not. I watched her go with Max and inhaled heavily when they slipped through the gap he made in the veil, only letting the breath out when the slice sealed shut behind them.

I took a step forward, heading for a chair, my head suddenly spinning. But when I reached my hand out, I missed the back of it, two of the same piece of furniture suddenly appearing before me. Strong hands grasped me on my right, small but firm on my left, the flick of a silver tail making me dizzy.

Sassafras's sharp voice was the last thing I heard. "She's going to pass out—"

And darkness, more engulfing even than sorcery's black heart, took me.

I woke to the touch of someone's fingers stroking my cheek. A soft moan escaped me, my body waking before my mind, the familiar heat and touch of magic so lovely I wanted to hug him close and kiss him until neither of us could breathe.

My eyes opened in a snap as I realized what I was feeling. Not sorcery, not with sorcery, but my demon power, back again, strong and stable with the thrumming darkness still pulsing beneath, my witch magic woven through it. And Ram, my darling Rameranselot, hovered above me, smiling, looking like himself, down to the tiny scar still marring his right cheek.

I touched the mark, the place where my blow had drawn blood, back before I knew anything of the Planeless and still under my grandfather's thumb. Ram caught my questing hand and brought it to his lips, kissing the skin in tingling touches, amber eyes heavy lidded.

"Welcome back," he said. And bent to kiss me.

"Ahem," Sassafras's voice broke through. I turned my head to find him crouched on my pillow, ears back, whiskers quivering. "If you two don't mind terribly, we have more important things to do."

I laughed and hugged him to me, pressing my lips to his furry brow, stroking his soft, round body to the tip of his tail. "We do," I said, meeting Ram's smiling eyes. "I take it the cure was a success?"

Sassafras wriggled free of me, swatting at my hands. "Of course," he said at his most haughty. "My father is a genius, after all."

I reached inside me, welcomed home the burning power of my demon magic, laughing out loud at the feeling of the connection between it and my sorcery. No longer a monster, but a savior, I welcomed her in, felt her combine with my waiting power. The surge of energy that raced through me made me gasp.

"He is," I said. "And now I have what I need to win."

I hoped.

Chapter Eighteen

I sat at the table, facing Raethnn and her people, with Zinnia on one side and Ram on the other. He seemed as fully recovered as I was, though I worried he might push himself too far, too soon. Sassafras perched in my lap, tail thrashing, while I filled everyone in on what I learned.

I was just finishing when Theridialis entered, leaning heavily on Bakari. My chair legs scraped the floor as I stood, Sass leaping to the table top, and rushed forward, my magic supporting the scientist. He sat heavily in a chair, smiling gently up at me, one hand touching my cheek in thanks.

"Thank you, dear," he said. "I'm fine, really. Just need a bit of rest." His face hardened. "But that can wait."

Shuffling feet, a nervous throat clearing and Portlish arrived, surrounded by Daeva. I was so tired suddenly of their secrecy and the way they still clung to their old ways,

I slammed power into his guards, driving them back and beckoning to the broken cook to come forward. He hobbled toward me rapidly to stand at Theridialis's side like a protective watchdog. The bruising on his face and the way he favored his already twisted body told me he hadn't had an easy time of it with Rutorith and the guards of the Seat, but at least he was in one piece.

"You're safe." I gripped his hand, smiling in relief. From the startled look on his face, he wasn't expecting me to give him a second thought.

"They thought me a mere inconvenience," Portlish bowed over our clasped hands. "A benefit of being one of my particular appearance." He seemed to physically morph, his face twisting into more grotesque visage, body's haphazard makeup worsening as he relaxed into a grinning, twisted and vacant waste of a demon. "Yessah, nossah." He wiped a dribble of drool from his chin as he righted himself to his usual, less twisted, form. "Simple enough to go unnoticed or be passed over as unimportant when you look like I do."

I wanted to weep for him. What a horrible life he must have had, growing up ignored and forgotten thanks to his appearance, but with a brilliant mind that captured every nuance around him. I squeezed gently and let his hand go, determined to do whatever I could for him to ensure he wasn't forced back into his old life as a cook for a crooked nectar dealer.

Theridialis patted Portlish's hand when it fell on his shoulder and he smiled. "My young, brilliant friend here might have fooled the guards, but he doesn't fool me." His eyes glittered with good nature. "In fact, he almost had it." Theridialis shifted slightly as though the chair made him uncomfortable and I wondered if his robe hid more damage than I'd seen yet. "He was so close, did you know?" The old scientist shook his head before I could answer. "Of course you do. He brought Ram out of the worst of it, didn't he?"

"Finally," Portlish said in his velvet voice, color rising in his face as he fought the praise Theridialis offered. "But not completely."

Sass's father just shrugged. "You were only missing one ingredient, my boy," he said, "and no one can fault you for not having access."

"Sorcery," I said, making the connection. "He didn't have access to sorcery."

Theridialis tapped his nose with his index finger, eyes bright. "Brilliant, as always," he said. "Yes, Meira. The final component."

"But you don't have it," I said. "Do you?"

He shook his head. "I didn't. But when Xeoniteridone captured me and dosed me, I did. And helped me understand what my own cure was missing." A hacking cough brought him to a halt a moment, the deep, wet contractions of his lungs making me very worried.

But he shook me off when I tried to offer him energy to heal, hand grasping mine. "I'm fine," he said. "I just need rest. After this is over."

I wished I could say otherwise, but he was right. "Explain this to me," I said. "From the beginning. The nectar suppresses demon magic, waking our sorcery."

"Correct." Theridialis immediately switched to teacher mode, his injuries and suffering seemingly forgotten. "Which would normally create a race of highly unruly creatures reverting to their own need for destruction."

"But that didn't happen," Syd said. "Why not?"

"Because Xeoniteridone possesses a particular power," Theridialis said. "One I can only assume Liander Belaisle cultivated on purpose. He is remarkably talented at coercion."

"Which he embedded in the nectar he had his people create," Portlish said.

"Also correct," Theridialis beamed up at the cook. "By suppressing demon power and opening our race to our sorcery, at the same time controlling the will of his targets through coercion, he was able to create a pliable mass from which he could not only draw power, but that he could use to sever the connections of the Node. He started slowly, as you know." Theridialis bowed his head to me. "But once he saw his plan was working, he increased his efforts until we are here, now, in the trouble we find ourselves."

"If we free our people from the nectar," I said, mind churning as I wrapped my thoughts around where to go from here, "will that also free their power and the coercion?"

"Portlish's tests finally freed Rameranselot of his thrall," Theridialis said. "So I can only assume the answer is yes."

"What about sorcery?" Syd looked worried. "Sorry, Meems, but I'm not sure giving demons free access to the dark magic is a great idea, especially when they are awake and aware."

"Nor am I," Max said. "Considering that is where we started in the first place, so many years ago."

"We can't worry about that now," I said. "Unless there's a way to cut them off again that won't complicate things?"

Raethnn didn't look hopeful. "It took the drach to shut off our race's ability last time, through the creation of the Node."

Max nodded. "Very true," he said. "If there is a way to rebuild it, we might be able to do so again." He didn't sound convinced. "It required the attention of my entire race and right now we are in the middle of a battle we are losing."

I had to make an executive decision. Once this was over, maybe we could find a new way to shut off demon sorcery. Until then, the more important problem was freeing my people first. "We'll cut down the trees we need to build that bridge when we get to it," I said. "Right now, we must have as much of the antidote as we can possibly muster."

"Already on it," Theridialis said. "Portlish and I will have what you need when you need it, I promise you."

I reached out and hugged Portlish. Our last meeting had been in the bowels of the Seat's cells, leaving me with more guilt to carry. "I'm sorry I left you behind."

He stiffened before softening and hugging me back. "Thank you, my Ruler," he said.

I leaned away and smiled, shaking my head. "Not Ruler now," I said. "Though, I plan to change that."

Meira. Ahbi's mental voice sounded strained. *As much as I'd like to allow you to continue this conversation, we're almost out of time. If you're going to act, you'd better do it now.*

The planes? I turned from Theridialis, stomach clenching, but ready to act.

I'm holding them together until you have the antidote assembled, she sent. *I don't want to see the Node fall before our people are free. But I can't do it much longer.*

Let the planes go, Grandmother, I sent. *Come back to me.*

I can't do that. She refused to allow me in when I tried to reach for her. *Just do what you have to, Meira. And don't worry about me.*

She cut me off then, disappearing into what remained

of the Node connection. Just the fact she told me not to worry set off so many alarm bells I knew there was a great deal to worry about. Nothing new there. But I finally stopped long enough to look that fear in the face again and I didn't like what I saw.

"The nectar you created for Xeoniteridone," I turned to Theridialis again. "Can you modify the controls out of it?"

"Why?" He frowned at me, hands twisting in his lap. "You don't need it, Meira."

"It gave me so much power." I felt my monster rumble agreement.

"Power you always had." Theridialis sighed, looking like an old demon at last, carrying his centuries with him on his face. "The nectar was only meant to ensure you weren't controlled by Xeoniteridone completely, to give you access to your mind when he thought you were under his sway. Nothing more."

"But…" I trailed off, touching my own magic, feeling the depth of it. "You're sure?"

He smiled at me, flicking his fingers in my direction. "I knew the nectar he asked me to make had to be for you. I was very careful to only augment what you had, not change it or make you dependent. My former mate did enough damage with her own experiments. You didn't need such from me, too." I flinched from the memory of Sekaniphestat and her attempt to use me to get to Dad. "I simply gave you what you needed in a way only you could use. But the power was yours to control all along. I only helped you find the way."

Was he right? I dove into my core, let it wash around me, touched the weaving of demon magic and sorcery, the swelling of energy powerful, so complete, I almost didn't recognize myself.

And then, I felt it. The soft and pulsing connection between planes. Like a road map of veins, running with sorcery and a hint of demon power. "I see it now," I said, almost breathless. "I see everything." I gestured to Sassafras as I emerged from within. "Come with me."

He didn't hesitate, leaping into my arms before I tore open the veil and stepped through into the Node room as though I did that sort of thing every day.

Well done, Ahbi's voice was stronger here. *You've learned to ride the veil like your sister.*

I have, I sent. *And none too soon. Grandmother, I can feel the connections now.*

Sassafras wriggled in my arms. *Show me.* I tried to, but he finally sighed. *I don't see anything.*

Part of the reason I brought you here, I sent, a little sad. *I wanted to be sure I was the only one.*

I need to wake my sorcery, the Persian growled.

Later, I sent. *For now, I need to ask Ahbi about the Node. Can you feel them, Grandmother? The other planes? That's how you found me, isn't it?*

Her mental voice was affirmative. *As soon as I rejoined the Node*, she sent. *They are separate, but the connection went on for so long, they left an imprint on each other. Like a phantom Node.*

Which means? Sassafras's ears twitched as he thought it through. *We can rebuild the Node using the existing connections?*

That's the hope, I sent to him with that emotion burning away inside me. *We won't have to work nearly as hard as the founders did. The network already exists. We just need the juice to pull them all together again.*

The power of Demonicon, Ahbi sent. *It contains a portion of every single plane. It's the last piece of the puzzle.*

Use it to call the planes together, I sent, *and sorcery to seal the deal again.*

Simple and brilliant, Sassafras sent. *But will it work?*

Only one way to find out. I hugged him. *I have to get the magic of Demonicon back. And more, I need help from the drach.*

True, Ahbi sent. *They were there when the Nodes were made, both successfully and not so much.*

But they are busy saving the Universe, Sass sent.

Still. I reached through the veil, amazed at how easy it now was. *If we can make this happen quickly and without too much fuss, their problems will go away with ours.*

I touched Syd's mind and felt her shock. *Meems, are you okay?*

More than that, I sent. *I have to talk to Max.*

I filled him in even though I could feel his attention

was divided between me and what he was doing. Glimpses of charred edges of veil showed through as he listened to what I had to say.

Here's what I need, I finished. *A drach on every separated plane, to deliver the antidote and to stand by to assist in reassembling the Node.*

You ask us to abandon our protection of the veil, he sent, though softly and with kindness.

I know what I'm asking, I sent. *But you yourself said when this is resolved it's likely the continuing damage will cease and you'll be able to finally put an end to it.*

True, he sent. *If I'm correct.*

Are you?

Silence followed my question. *I do not know*, Max sent at last. *But we cannot go on this way forever. So we must try something and your plan seems the best alternative. We will assemble on Demonicon and take possession of the antidote. The drach are with you, Ruler.*

Now, if only I could assure myself my plan wasn't going to be a horrible failure and his faith in it wasn't unfounded.

ChAPTER NINETEEN

I returned with Sassafras to the Daeva, to deliver the good—or scary—news the drach would be arriving literally a moment before the air of the room burst open and the human-formed dragons stepped through.

Not all of them, clearly—perhaps fifty or so. They all had the same basic appearance, diamond eyed and gray skinned, dressed in long, gray robes. But the longer they stood there, the more diverse their faces became to me as Max and Syd stepped forward to speak.

"My people are ready," Max said. "Command us."

I shared what I'd learned, what Sass, Ahbi and I had deducted. Raethnn's scowl told me she wasn't a hundred percent behind my plan, but I didn't give a crap at the moment. I had a world to save and her secrecy had almost cost us everything.

Theridialis appeared, looking a little stronger, Portlish

on one side and Ram on the other.

"The antidote is ready," the scientist said in a grim tone. "Made for airborne delivery. A blanketed dispersal should reach every demon on each plane within a few minutes."

"And the drach stand by to deliver it," Max said.

I let the pair come together to plot the logistics, meeting Ram's gaze across the room. He left Theridialis to come to my side, standing just behind me as I made my next announcement.

"I'm going upstairs," I said. "And I'm going to take my throne back."

Raethnn calmed a little, perhaps because this was something she could tackle, too. "You will not go alone," she said. "The Daeva will come with you."

Bakari twitched. "Leader," he said.

She cut him off with a sharp jerk of one hand. "We have been too long in the darkness," she said. "If this has proved anything to us, it is our ways are no longer valid or doing the job we need to do." She nodded to me, skin tightening as she frowned. "It's time our people worked together with our Ruler to ensure the safety of all."

I bowed my head back. "I appreciate it," I said, softening toward her. After all, she'd spent centuries living this way. It couldn't be easy to step into the light. "And you will always have my support and gratitude. On one condition."

Raethnn's arched brow swept toward her hairline. "My Ruler?"

"I get to kill Henemordonin," I said, blood thirst rising as my monster hummed.

The Daeva leader smiled so viciously I was suddenly grateful she was on my side.

"As you wish," she said.

Did I ever.

Ram caught my arm gently as I turned to go. I met his eyes, shook my head.

"You're not up to this," I spoke softly, keeping it between us.

"Don't ask me to stay out of it." His amber eyes darkened, face angry. "Meira, I won't. You need me." Was that a question in his statement? Was he asking me if I needed him?

I hugged him, arms tight around his chest, remembering briefly the touch of Elphremantic and hoping to someday purge that memory from my mind. Holding Ram, feeling his arms around me, helped a great deal, though my monster hummed and nudged his sorcery, making things a little awkward.

"I will always need you," I said into his strong chest. "Always. But you've been through so much, more than any of us."

Ram pushed me back, grip firm, but not hurtful. "I'm coming with you," he said. "You'll have to tie me up and leave me under full guard to keep me away."

Ahbi sighed dramatically. *Oh, for the sake of the Node,* she sent. *Just let the boy go with you already.*

I giggled into my hands at the absurdity of it all. "Fine," I said at last. "Since Ahbi seems to think it's a good idea."

Ram bowed to the empty air. "My thanks."

He's such a dear, she sent.

"Are we using magic?" Zinnia came to stand with me, her hands full of clothing. I suddenly realized I was still in a state of undress and gratefully took them from her.

"No," I said. "We'll take the stairs. I don't want him to know we're coming until it's too late."

A quick change into my favorite tight suit and draped gown and we were heading for the staircase. I reached for Sequoia and Jabuticabron the moment we began our ascent. They both embraced me with happy excitement when I touched their minds and were waiting for us at the top when we emerged into my quarters.

I was certain Sequoia would choke me to death when she hugged me, scooping up her furry brother at last when Jabut fell to one knee before me and hung his head. I cupped his face in my hands and firmly kissed his brow, forcing him to rise.

"My friends," I said. "Where is Pagomaris?"

She stepped forward from where she half-hid behind the siblings, hands in fists at her sides. "My Ruler," she choked out.

I hugged her, too, feeling her shaking, knowing then, despite the role she played, she really did care for me.

"I thought you lost," she whispered. "After losing Ahbi… I didn't think I could survive your death, too."

I let her go and kissed her cheek. Her smile wavered, touching the spot with her fingertips.

"I'm fine," I said. "But I do have one problem." My fists settled on my hips, one cocked to the side, a little grin on my lips. "It would appear someone is sitting in my seat and I want it back."

Pagomaris clapped her hands like a little girl before composing herself. "My Ruler," she curtsied. "Shall I dress you?"

"No," I said. "I'm going the way I am. And they're damned well going to like it or I'm pushing the lot of them over the edge."

My court. There'd be a massive power reshuffle when this was over. They wanted law changes? I'd give them changes. First on the roster, no more fighting for position. We'd see how they liked the new me.

"We can sneak you in through the lab entry," Sequoia said.

"No," I said with a grin. "I have a better idea. This requires an entrance." I spun and left my quarters before anyone could stop me, stomping my way down the familiar hall to the elevator. I was already on it by the time my friends made it halfway down the hall and I only waited a moment for Sassafras to bound his way to my side, Ram in a rush behind him, before ascending.

The others could catch the next ride. I had work to do.

I felt my grandfather's power the moment I touched foot to the floor of the throne room. A chorus of gasps met with my appearance and, to my surprise, looks of sudden hope and joy at the sight of me. That was a switch, though I held off my sympathy. Besides, I was too focused on the pretender sitting on my throne to care what the court thought of me.

He stood, the power of Demonicon battling him in flames as he pointed at me.

"Arrest her!"

I wonder if he was shocked the guards in the room remained rooted in place. Of course, my power held them there, not allowing them to act, but they also didn't seem all that interested in fighting me in the first place. I took it as a good sign.

Even better when, his grim face drawn in regret, Rutorith bowed his head to me.

My grandfather's rage wavered with fear as I strode to the bottom of the dais. I heard others coming behind me, knew my friends had caught up. I ignored them, glaring my fury at Henemordonin.

It was my turn to point as his arm fell to his side.

"Pretender," I said. "Give me my power back, or I'll kill you right now."

He attacked me, or tried to, throwing magic at me. Demonicon's power still struggled against him, his sorcery tied up and convoluted thanks to the battle he raged. Regardless of his condition, he would still have lost, but it was imminently satisfying to see him fall to the very magic he'd stolen from me.

"Even Demonicon herself rejects you, Henemordonin." I crossed my arms over my chest, opened my full power and let him feel what I'd become. His gasp killed the last of his arrogance and pure terror crossed his face. "Step down and I'll go easy on you. Maybe."

"He won't do that." I snarled at the familiar voice, turned to find Elphremantic emerging from behind Second Seat. I was shocked myself when he firmly placed himself on the smaller throne. "He is Ruler and you are a wanted criminal."

I chose to ignore the snotty ass and refocused on my grandfather.

"You know it's the right thing to do," I said. "Give it back and let me fix this. Or I will kill you and no one will stop me."

He hesitated, and for the first time, I saw the old demon my grandfather was, just as wasted as Raethnn after years of fighting an unnecessary battle with the truth. Beaten and pathetic, cornered by his own greed, his face reflected the conflict in him. And I was sure he would give me what I wanted without a fight.

I didn't count on Elphremantic interfering, not that it mattered any. He rose from his throne and put himself between me and my grandfather.

"You'll have to go through me to get to Ruler," he said.

Did he just…? Excellent. I grinned, teeth bared, and gathered my power.

"Perfect," I said, climbing one stair to get in his face. I know he expected me to use magic against him. That's why it was so satisfying to pull my arm back and hit him in the mouth with all the strength I could muster.

Chapter Twenty

The blow, backed by my magic, took him in the jaw, square and solid, lifting him from his feet and sending him back into Henemordonin. My grandfather cursed as Elphremantic landed on him, sending them both sprawling backward onto First Seat.

I shook out my hand, still grinning. "Oh, sorry," I said, "were you thinking I hit like a girl?" Magic pooled around me, the touch of Demonicon's power begging me to release it so it could return. But I wanted Henemordonin to give it back on purpose, by choice. I wanted him beaten and begging me for his life. And I would do whatever necessary to make him grovel on his hands and knees at my feet before he returned what was mine.

Elphremantic regained his feet, roughly brushing at his clothing, dabbing at the blood running from his lip.

"You bitch," he snarled. "I'll crush you and make you my slave."

"Tried that already, didn't you, little boy?" I prodded him with energy. "How did that work out for you?"

He howled, hands extended, blackness pouring from them to engulf me. I brushed at his sorcery, waving it aside like a noxious cloud and registered the sudden fear on his face.

"Well, that was rather a weak and useless effort," I said. "Care to try again?" My demon fire burned his feet in a rush of magic, sending him dancing sideways, eyes huge. "I'm guessing you were thinking I wouldn't be much of a target. A crippled and contained opponent who couldn't fight back?" My monster roared, diving for him, bringing him to the ground. Licks of magic tasted him, sucked at his power while he writhed and fought. "I'd say pick on someone your own size, Elphremantic, but no one is as small and pathetic as you."

He gasped for air. "I'll kill you."

"You've already tried your best," I said. "I'm not here for you, though I'll happily drain you. I'm here, as Ruler, to put an end to your father."

Elphremantic fell still. "He's not here."

"I highly doubt that," I said. "Or, he's watching, at least. While taking a break from doing his best to create his own power of Demonicon." The last piece of that puzzle fell into place. "That's his goal, the reason for the separation, isn't it?" Of course it was. "He wants to rebuild the Node, but, like me, he'd need to have all the power of Demonicon to do it. And since he allowed Henemordonin to keep my magic, he had to be assembling his own. And could only do so after the Node gave up the planes or else risk having it fight against him."

Both Elphremantic and my grandfather looked shocked, all the confirmation I needed, though I wondered if Henemordonin actually knew what Xeoniteridone was up to all along.

"He'll soon have everything he needs," Elphremantic panted. "More powerful than any magic you think you possess. He could have taken the magic of Demonicon from both of you any time wanted." Elphremantic wheezed a laugh. "But he wanted more, bigger pieces of the planes, and the only way to do that was to take them himself." He struggled briefly again, panting as he quit. "And when he's done, he'll crush you, Meira, like a worm and give me the remains to play with." Again with the lip licking. I was going to liberate him of his tongue once and for all, the moment this was over.

My grandfather looked suddenly ill. "It's true, then." He turned to face the slim demon. So he hadn't known? "This has all been a lie?"

"You old fool," Elphremantic hissed at him. "As if Father ever intended you allow you to keep the throne or any kind of power. He will drain you, too, and use your body for a toy while the new Demonicon rises around us." Fanatical zeal burned in his face, spit flying from his lips. He looked as insane as his father. "You will all burn in the fires of the Seat and we will be victorious."

I squashed him harder, making him groan. "Tired of you talking," I said. "You can stop now." It wasn't as if he was giving me new information, and I really was sick of the sound of his voice.

My grandfather sagged forward, falling to his knees, meeting my gaze with his hands stretched out before him, held out to me. "I didn't know," he choked his words. "I swear it, Meira. I see my failings, my pride." His hands rose to cover his face. "I only wanted a better life for all demons." He dropped his arms, expression broken, hurt. "I was under their influence. He told me no one would be hurt, that this was for the greater good of our entire world. I truly believed it would be so." Shoulders slumping, he sagged, an old demon lost. "Forgive me, granddaughter. I knew not what I did."

My slow clap broke the silence following his little speech. "Brilliant," I said. "The Oscar goes to. But the trouble with your whole 'confession', Henemordonin?" His eyes lifted to meet mine. "You knew all along what was happening, even if the end game wasn't what you expected. You knew Xeoniteridone was using mind control and nectar to control our people, to manipulate and enslave them. And to strip them of their magic while freeing their sorcery so he could take our world apart." The entire court, all their waving feathers and elaborate clothing tipped with silver spikes stared in horror and broken will at my grandfather as I turned to face them. "He knew. And so," I pointed at the lot of them, "did you." Guilty starts, protests, but I cut them off. "There are those of you who supported him, who were complicit. Who formed a shadow government to remove my power." More guilt, this time apparent as those who weren't part of it stepped away from those who were. Children and wives against husbands and grandparents. I snarled in savage fury at them, wanting nothing more than to wash my hands. But they were my responsibility now. And I'd deal with them, one way or another.

"Consider yourselves served notice," I said. "The minute this crisis is resolved, I'm taking names and action."

I spun away from them to their soft cries of hopelessness, hardening myself against them. Let them stew in that for the remainder of this drama. I had other things to worry about.

I hadn't counted on Elphremantic's slipperiness, and underestimated him. The distraction of my little lecture eased up my control over him. As I shifted back toward my grandfather, I realized only then the slimy bastard was free and, eyes wide, looked full in the face of an oncoming mass of magic.

My shields slammed into place, but the power never hit me. To my shock, Henemordonin leaped to his feet the moment before the mass of energy was about to strike and stepped in front of it with a roar of anger.

I stood rooted as he staggered and then spun. "DECEIVER!" My grandfather threw himself at Elphremantic, the pair falling to the ground and rolling around, fists and feet flying, snarling at each other, bits and pieces of power flaring, but their hatred for each other manifesting in a more physical confrontation.

My energy pulled them apart, Henemordonin panting, wiping at blood on his cheek while Elphremantic tried to go after him again.

"You're even more of an old fool than Father thought," the young demon growled.

"Yes," Xeoniteridone's voice carried to me, spun me around as he strode up the center aisle past the cringing court. "Yes, he was. And it's time to take care of him once and for all." Xeon smiled at me. "Hello, my dear," he said. "So lovely to see you again. Shall we end a world today?"

Before I could respond, the throne room flooded with demons, the Planeless, emerging through countless black holes created by sorcery. The court squealed as a whole, rushing to bunch into a circle in the middle of the room, sparkly clothing and waving bouffants making them appear as a gaggle of desperate birds trying to flee a predator and just getting in each other's way.

Shocking me yet again, my grandfather rushed forward and put himself in the line of fire, between me and the leader of the Planeless.

"It wasn't supposed to happen this way." His voice warped and crackled, hands shaking at his sides as Henemordonin addressed his former ally. "You promised me no one would be harmed. But it's nothing like you said it would be." His fists hit his thighs. "Nothing!"

Xeoniteridone's lazy grin told me my grandfather had been played just as much as I had, enough to soften me slightly toward him. Not enough to save his soul, but maybe enough to keep him alive.

"How did we end up here?" Henemordonin turned toward me, hands reaching for me again, this time with utter honesty in his face. "Spiraling down into darkness with every agreement? I am an old, stupid, arrogant demon, my granddaughter. I have led us to destruction, willingly. And when it became too much, it was far too late." He again dropped his hands, regret and grief pulling his face into a caricature of himself. "I was in so deep, I couldn't break free. I kept hoping things would change, that this would all work out in the end." He shook his head. "I'm sorry, I truly am. I should have seen who I was working with instead of falling for his lies about unity and peace for our people."

"But Henemordonin," Xeoniteridone interrupted. "I have brought those things." There was laughter in his words as his people herded mine into a pod of fear.

"Liar," Henemordonin snarled. "You've brought what Meira said. Slavery and silence. You've crippled our people instead of saving them."

"But I'm not done yet." Xeoniteridone winked at me. "Not by a long shot."

My grandfather turned full around and took my hands in his before I could stop him. The power of Demonicon flowed outward and into me, making me gasp as he thrust it toward me.

"May you use it more wisely than I ever could," he whispered before turning back to Xeoniteridone with a frantic expression. "Defeat us now, evil one!"

I felt the magic settle inside me like an old friend, integrating perfectly with my demon power and the monster of my sorcery. For a heady moment, it seemed as if I were a goddess, those before me merely petty irritations I could easily squish under my boots.

Meira! Ahbi's voice cut through my instant of divinity. *Pay attention!*

The cult leader was clearly angry at this turn of events because when he laughed at my grandfather, he did so with a terrible edge to his amusement. "So weak, Henemordonin," he said. "As always. Unable to even control a little girl, you finally cracked. I'm not surprised."

Elphremantic finally spoke up. "Four years wasted on this sack of crap," he snarled at his father. "When we could have acted."

Xeoniteridone waved one hand at his angry son. "No matter. I'm ready now." I felt the immense power in him, the match to mine, though not complete, not yet. There were three planes left for him to harvest from, planes Ahbi held together yet.

Barely, she sent.

Tell Max and the others to act now, I sent. *Send out the antidote. I want it dispersed immediately.*

Done, she sent. *Be careful.*

Meems! Syd's voice cut through. I could feel her with Max, floating over one of the lost planes. They'd gone together to oversee the dispersal of the antidote. But she felt now like she thought she'd made the wrong choice. *I'm coming.*

I've got this. I shut her down as Xeoniteridone raised his arms over his head, his staff glowing with white light.

"You may have power," he said, "but you don't have what you need to stop me, Meira. I hold sway over the magic of our people, our true power, sorcery. And you only have your own paltry ability to draw from." He cackled, like an old woman. "While you fight to stop me, I will absorb all the magic of our planes like no demon ever has. And when I'm done, I'll feast on the veil itself and I will rule the Universe."

CHAPTER TWENTY ONE

The air crackled beside me, my sister stepping through. She was laughing.

"Heard that one before," she said.

I almost laughed with her as Xeoniteridone, clearly furious with my sister's appearance and jab at his plans, threw up a large, vibrating shield between himself and her.

"You really need to learn to mind your own business," he said. "You're not as important as you seem to think you are." His glittering eyes settled on Max who had slipped through the veil with Syd. "How's your little fight in the veil going, drach?" Nasty, bitter laughter escaped the white-haired demon. "I hope you're finding it entertaining."

My hands ached from being fisted at my sides. "You knew this would happen." The damage to the veil didn't seem to bother him in the least.

"Of course I did." His staff's crystal sparked, his smirk stirring my anger further. "When I discovered the damage already done to the veil, I made sure my manipulations of Demonicon's power trickled out to aggravate the issue." He waved his hand at Max as though dismissing him as unimportant. "Simplicity itself to keep the drach from interfering with my plans. Their sense of responsibility is truly pathetic. And predictable."

Max's growling told me Xeoniteridone had hit a soft spot in the normally calm and level-headed drach leader.

The cult master raised his staff over his head, his insanity showing as he laughed once again.

"You are all fools, slow and incompetent." White fire burst from the crystal on the top of his staff, pouring sparks over him. "You could never attain my brilliance or keep up with my plans. I've been controlling and manipulating you for years without your knowledge." His tone turned to a disappointed teacher. "Really," he said. "Could you have been easier to influence?"

Henemordonin groaned, hands over his face. "All my fault," he said.

Xeoniteridone nodded, smiling his benevolent smile. "Yes," he said. "It certainly looks that way. And I'm sure Meira will be happy to reward you for your part in my plotting once she's mine completely and firmly on the First Seat once again."

"You seem to think you have this all worked out," Syd said, crossing her arms over her chest. While my heart pounded with worry Xeoniteridone really had more cards to show, she seemed unimpressed.

He snapped his teeth at her, flipping from kindly religious leader to crazy psychopath in the blink of an eye. "I may be like you," he said. "I may have a sorcerer father and a demon mother, but I am so much more than you will ever be." His power rumbled around him, shaking the top of the Seat, making the domed shields overhead vibrate and flare. "I have no constraints, untethered by conscience or empathy. I see what must be done and I am doing it." He shook his head at Syd, smiling once again. "I watched with interest, and then boredom, as you and that useless girl you fought—Ameline, was it?—failed over and over to put an end to one another. And when you finally killed her, it was over a child." He blew air through his lips. "You could have enslaved her, compelled her to serve you. Instead, you gave away the power you took from her. Gave it away." He seemed suddenly baffled. "I knew then you were no match for me. And that my plan would work perfectly."

"It still took you four years," Syd said, sounding bored herself. She even picked at a hang nail while I gaped at her for prodding him. "If you're so amazing, why did it take you so long?"

His staff came down on the floor with a crack of

thunder, the shielding above us sparking like lightning in response. For a heartbeat, the wards collapsed. I was instantly on my knees, the pressure of the wind and the thinness of the air driving me to the polished floor. I gasped for a breath, looked up to see Xeoniteridone standing, facing off with my sister and Max. The sight forced me to my feet, sorcery sucking at the power around me even as the magic of Demonicon did its job and rebuilt the shields.

Syd looked ruffled but unharmed, Max's anger bare on his face. The entire court seemed to be sobbing, male and female alike, while my grandfather panted for air, head bowed.

Xeoniteridone gestured to me with irritation. "I wanted those shields down," he said, pushing against my power.

"I think they're fine the way they are." I didn't bother pushing back, not because I didn't want to fight him, but because Sassafras and Ahbi reached out to me at the exact same moment.

Don't let him see how powerful you are, Sass sent.

Hide, Ahbi added.

Smart. Though I was ready to go at him now, immediately.

Not yet, Ahbi sent. *Let the Node fall. Then your demon power, at least, will be equal.*

You think my sorcery is stronger than his? I remembered

fighting him off, saving Bilhaeder, if temporarily.

I'm sure of it, Sassafras sent as Ahbi's mind hugged mine.

Be ready for it, she sent and left me.

Xeoniteridone backed off without really pushing me, smile gentle yet again. "You may have your little protections," he said, voice growing in volume as he began to pontificate. I was used to Henemordonin's grand performances, so watching the Planeless leader wasn't all that impressive. "No matter what you do, Meira, you are no match for me. I was made to rule." He strode toward me, closing the distance while his cult followers tightened their control over the gathered court.

Syd tried to move, but I snapped in her head. *Leave him to me.*

She shot me a look that seemed to disagree with my request, but held her ground as Xeoniteridone finally came to a halt a mere ten feet from me. Close enough I could see the crazy behind his sweet smile.

"I will own this Universe," he said. "And when I do, you will regret fighting against your new master."

"I knew you were nuts," I said, mimicking Syd's casual tone, "but I had no idea you had a God complex. Way to be a whack job, Xeon."

Was it really that simple to trigger a response from him? It seemed so. All pretense of kindness and warmth left him, his snarl returning, eyes burning with fire.

"I will suck you dry myself," he said, leaning forward. "And when I'm through, I'll give your empty shell to my son for his toy."

"You'll try," I said, the quiver in my belly, fear that appeared from the start of this confrontation, fading away. Warmth filled me as I drew in my magic, feeling as though I were finally whole as the power of Demonicon, my sorcery and my own personal demon magic combined to flood me with strength. "And you'll fail."

I suppose I shouldn't have been surprised my grandfather didn't share my newfound confidence in my abilities. He staggered to my side, trying to yet again put himself between me and Xeoniteridone.

"I'm your true target," he said, desperation clear in his voice.

"You," Xeoniteridone said, sweeping his staff forward, "are no longer of use to anyone." The tip of his staff brushed against Henemordonin's chest. I heard my grandfather gasp, watched him half-turn toward me, hand clutching the spot, eyes huge. It wasn't until I noticed the white flames rising from between his fingers I realized the touch of the staff did more damage than it appeared.

Without thinking, I reached out with my sorcery and devoured the flames. The power behind them flooded the darkness with light, sending quivers of delight through me. Henemordonin staggered to the side, out of the line of fire as Xeoniteridone frowned at me with hesitation.

"How did you do that?" He shook his staff at me. "You shouldn't have been able to do that."

I tasted the fire, now part of my magic. "Delicious," I said. "More, please."

chapter twenty two

Xeoniteridone's full pause of concern made me smile. Even more so when I felt Ram's mind touch mine.

The drach have completed the delivery, he sent. *The antidote is now away.*

Excellent. Knowing things were about to get ugly, I threw a net of power around Xeoniteridone and myself, much as I would if I were engaging in a battle for Plane status, only many times stronger than normal. Xeoniteridone registered my act as I cut us off from the rest of the room with a sudden grin.

"You weaken your power," he said, suddenly sly, shifting his weight forward, staff at the ready. "To protect those who care nothing for you and barely deserve to lick your boots."

"Think what you like," I said, letting my magic out to pool at my feet, climbing like a living vine around my legs, rising behind me in a wall of flame, the amber tinted with white—thanks to him and his odd power—and black. "But maybe you should consider I have the strength to spare, Xeon."

That made him hesitate again. My turn to laugh in his face.

"Scared yet?" I prodded him with power, using his own to dig tiny holes in his shields. What was so special about those white flames of his? They reminded me of the black ones of my sorcery, but different, more pure. "You should be."

He snarled like an animal as his staff flared. "We'll see how cocky you are," he said, "with your world in shambles around you." I felt the surge of sorcery, knew what was coming, but still wasn't prepared when I felt the last three planes vibrate along the edges of their connection.

Meira. Ahbi's voice whispered deep inside me. *It's happening now.*

Grandmother! I reached for her, tried to hold onto her as the last planes began to part.

My darling girl, she sent, pain in her mental voice, *be well and think of me with kindness.* Her words ended abruptly, my magic trying to hold her, cut off by the wailing sound of her agony before it, too, finished in as though cut off.

My ears rang from the sudden silence, my body tense as I waited for the end of everything. It never came. Utter quiet descended as, high above, the two other suns flared with light and vanished.

Xeoniteridone laughed, breaking the stillness. "It is done!" He spun in a circle, staff glowing. "I have succeeded!"

Meira! Ram's voice reached me. *It's working! We're receiving word from the drach—our people are waking up and fighting against their handlers.*

The cure worked. Now all I needed to do was put the Node back together before Xeoniteridone could act. Easy, sure thing.

He turned to me, a slight frown on his face, his exultation dying as he seemed to realize something was wrong. "What have you done?"

I flashed my teeth at him, reaching for Max. "Who has the power, now? Turns out your little network of sorcery, stolen from my people, had a weak spot." *I need to touch them all,* I sent to the drach. *But I need help.*

You shall have it. He connected with my mind and, through him, I felt the drach, the network of massive minds waiting for his command. *Use us as you wish.*

My mind almost fractured as I seized on their consciousnesses, so many of them, so much power, more than I'd ever felt before. Flashing images overlaid each other, as all the planes became visible to me through their eyes. I pushed myself forward, using the drach for boost, to cast a giant holographic image of myself in the sky over the waking demons' heads. So weird, hard to focus, seeing multiple layers, hundreds of them, all mashed together. But I leaned heavily on Max for support as I sent my message.

And showed my people who Xeon really was. Played out for them the last few minutes, his desire to own the Universe, how he'd treated them like puppets, stealing their power, suppressing their demon magic. Their shock, the touch of their returned energy, rejuvenated the power of Demonicon. And, through Max and the drach, through the magic I held from all planes, I touched each and every heart of each and every demon.

And they roared their support of me so loudly I thought Ostrogotho would echo from it despite the separation.

"No!" Xeoniteridone's staff came forward, flashed, but the white flames simple absorbed into me, feeding me further. I knew now where the white fire came from. Stolen from the spirits of my people, their sorcery no longer the blackness of empty hunger, but altered, shifted by his manipulations and the nectar he used to control them. It gave me a glimmer of hope, the starving, gaping need not present any longer. Had he given us a gift without knowing it? I smiled at him, though I barely saw him, still with my people.

"This is the demon you would have lead you," I said, both out loud and through my holograms. "This is the lying, deceitful demon who treats you like a means to his own evil end." I cracked open his mind with a swift thrust before he could stop me, using his own magic, funneling it through the staff and into him. The chaos and fury and utter hate that lived in him echoed inside me, carried to all demonkind.

The final straw. They rejected him as a people, in a single rush of power, filling me with their support and more—with the magic they had within them, giving willingly a portion of themselves where once only a winning battle would earn such a prize. And I swelled with their gift, until I felt I would never be able to contain it.

It was crisply clear, now, the connections between planes, still fresh and waiting to be reassembled. I touched the lines of the edges of Ostrogotho, the sizzle of magic, lonely for the planes that made it whole, burning white and clean. But I also knew, then, no matter the loss of the Node, no matter the separation of my race, I had what I needed to hold them together because, as a people, they gave it to me.

My vision returned to me, though I remained linked with the planes, my focus on Xeoniteridone. He was bent over his staff, coughing blood onto his pristine white robe. When he looked up, his face was a mess of crimson, running from his eyes, his ears, his nose, trickling from the corners of his twisted mouth.

"Sorry about that," I said. "Hope I didn't hurt you too badly."

He spit blood at me, wiping his face on his robe, smears of bright red marring the perfection of it. So much for the power he used to keep it clean.

"No matter," he said, choking on more blood. "I will rebuild the Node after I take your power from you and use your demons as siphons to drain magic from the veil." Was he really that insane he still thought he could win? Or did he have more up his now-filthy sleeves I didn't know about? "And when I am powerful enough, I will challenge Creator and rule everything!"

I touched his magic, needing to know if I'd missed anything. And realized I had.

His Demoniconian power was complete. He must have stolen parts of the last three planes during the separation while I was busy with my people. Did it matter? I had no idea.

When he raised his staff and pointed it at me, I knew I was about to find out.

Instead of attacking me directly, though, he whipped his arm upward and thrust the crystal toward the heavens. The sun's light died so quickly I spun and looked up, air leaving my lungs in a rush as a black cloud covered the sky, blotting out the brightness of the large star illuminating Ostrogotho. Through the connection to my people, I felt the sudden panic in the residents of this plane, their terror on the edge of a fear-filled rampage.

It took everything I had to soothe them, suddenly supported by the souls of the rest of my race who offered comfort and strength. How strange to feel my rebellious and angry people join together, without animosity, in a single cause. Perhaps I was wrong about demonocracy. Thanks to Xeoniteridone's meddling, it was now possible demons could find a way to live in peace and without constant battle. But that was a contemplation for another time.

I turned back to find the Planeless leader vibrating with magic, his sorcery the source of the black cloud. It would have been simple to counter him, but I had a feeling I'd be needing all of my power, so I let him use his to try to distract me.

From the savage rage on his face, the reappearance of the sun, I knew I'd guessed correctly. "You think yourself clever," he said.

"Smarter than you." I pointed upward. "At least I'm not playing games like a fearful child." This was it. I felt his tension, knew our final battle was a heartbeat away. And I just couldn't resist one last cut. "I'm going to really enjoy tossing you to the fires of the Seat. Bet that hair of yours lights up real pretty."

He howled at me and attacked.

In the background, I felt the rush of air as more sorcerers appeared, saw enough out of the corner of my eye to know it was the Daeva, not more Planeless supporters of Xeoniteridone, there to do battle with the cult. I let them have their fun, mostly because I didn't have much choice.

I might have been stronger than him, but Xeoniteridone wasn't an opponent to be taken lightly. The moment he attacked, he slithered to the right, then the left, slippery and deceitful. It seemed like every time I tried to counter his attack he slipped from my grasp and hit me hard where I least expected. My sorcery writhed, starving to devour him, while the power of Demonicon tried over and over to flatten him against the stone and pound him into submission. I continued to hear the collective howling of my people as their magic, now fed into mine, raged against the one who brought them so low.

Panting and frustrated, I reeled back from a cunning blow near my head, a clap of sound so loud it staggered me. He was faster than I, coming at me from the other side with sorcery this time, trying to siphon off some of the power my people gave me. Barely in time to prevent him, I threw up a shield between us, if only to give myself a moment to breathe.

And caught an unexpected blow to my feet, sweeping them out from under me. Not from Xeoniteridone, this time, but, as I saw when I turned to catch myself on both hands, from Elphremantic. He had somehow wormed his way under the shielding I used to protect the others from the battle and used his cowardly cunning to attack me when I wasn't paying attention.

Xeoniteridone ignored his son, coming to tower over me as I fought to scramble back and regain my feet. But he was quicker than me and I found myself at the top of the dais stairs, my back pressed to the base of my throne, as the tall and terrible cult leader leaned forward, his staff at the ready.

"Little girl," he said, sweetness dripping from his words. "All that power at your disposal and you refuse to commit it. And that, Meira, is why you failed."

Was he right? Was I afraid to let go completely?

"Step away from her." Ram's familiar voice made me tremble. I looked past Xeoniteridone to find my love with his arm around Elphremantic's neck, power tightening at the writhing demon's throat. "Or I'll kill your son."

Xeoniteridone didn't hesitate. With an absent flick of his fingers, he turned his back. "Then kill him," he said, so casually I gaped up at him in shock. "He's of no further use to me anyway."

Elphremantic cried out. "Father, please!"

The cult leader ignored him, focused on me once again. But Ram's distraction had given me the moment I needed to gather my wits, so when Xeoniteridone gathered his power to attack, I was already countering him.

Using his own tactics, but better. I divided the three powers I had control of and hit him with a triple-pronged attack. The base of his power gave under the sweeping blow of my personal magic, demon tied to my old, familiar—if no longer dominant—witch magic, exploding upward beneath him even as my sorcery hit him full in the chest, eating its way through his shields toward the flickering white flames. And, with all the strength I could muster, I landed a blow to his head with the power of Demonicon, swinging it like a sledgehammer.

I expected success, but not the spectacular result. Xeoniteridone's body launched upward before halting in mid-air, suspended as a black spear pierced his chest. He spun in a circle on that pivot-point, like a wheel of fortune, head rocking to the side and back from the blow of my power.

My sorcery gulped his magic while he threw the last of what he had outward and through my shields. Not an attack, but a call to action, his coercion as strong as ever.

I realized, then, his final source of energy needed to be cut off and, with a snapping crack of power, I separated him from the Planeless gathered, still fighting off the Daeva, leaving Xeoniteridone alone and unsupported.

My magic released him, dropping him to the ground with a heavy thud, the back of his head bouncing against the floor. I dove at him physically, one platform boot in the center of his chest, pinning him down as I breathed my sorcery into his face. The white flames from his staff licked around me, roared an instant. I savored their flavor, sharp and minty, before swallowing them whole, taking back the altered power of my people's sorcery from him.

With a gun-shot like retort, the crystal on the top of his staff shattered to the sound of Xeoniteridone's wail of denial.

"Nice try," I grinned in his face. "Now, let's see if the rest of you is as delicious."

He fought me, or tried to, and though I knew by pulling in his power I took on the flavor of who he was, I didn't hesitate or pause, draining him dry, faster and faster as his will faded and his ability to counter me died.

When I was done, his empty eyes stared up at me, mouth slack, a trail of drool trickling outward and into his white hair. The remains of him wriggled inside me, still trying to fight, but I smothered him in the magic at my disposal and listened with satisfaction to his soul's final death wail as I stood slowly, standing over him, before lifting my face to the sky and roaring my victory.

And all the demons of Demonicon roared with me.

chapter twenty three

I let the shield fall at last, the Daeva, led by Raethnn, coming forward to seize the empty shell of Xeoniteridone and relieve Ram of Elphremantic's wailing, quivering form.

"My Ruler." The desperate son of my fallen enemy tried to catch my attention. "Please, forgive me! It was all my father's idea. I was under his sway—"

"Save it." Ram shoved him a little harder than was necessary, Elphremantic falling into Bakari's not-so-gentle hands. "She's not interested."

I really wasn't. And not just because I still had a big job ahead of me, either. It would be a pleasure to see the slim demon who deceived me stripped of power. I might even let Ram take care of it personally.

My sorcery grumbled, hungry again.

I looked up, met my sister's eyes. She seemed

nervous, agitated, but when I gestured for her to come forward, she came at me with a rush and hugged me tight.

"Nice job, sis," she said. "Way to beat the bad guys."

I hugged her back. "More to do," I said.

She nodded, leaning away, touching my face, my shoulder with shaking hands. "You're okay?"

"Was there ever any doubt?" We laughed together, both of us quivering from the release of tension, though from the sparkling moisture in her eyes she really didn't think it was funny.

Max joined us as the Planeless, now reduced thanks to the loss of Xeoniteridone and the network he shared with them, were firmly and painfully rounded up by the Daeva.

"It's time to rebuild what was undone," he said in his rumbling voice.

I could still feel the drach, the planes, my people. They waited, their own cult members defeated and awaiting my ruling. My magic hummed, ready and willing as I flowed back through Max and into the veil.

I could see this time, without help, the darkness lit with lines separating all the planes. The demon ones glowed with amber fire, standing out from the rest of the vast, seemingly endless network, because of the brightness of their fire.

It only hit me then the absence of Ahbi. I reached for her, desperate now my mind made the loss connection, but found nothing.

She may yet be saved, Max sent. *As might Mabel.* More guilt and fear came to me now the main battle was over. I could worry about those I cared about and not put Demonicon ahead of them any longer. *But only once the Node is recreated.*

My sorcery wriggled when I harnessed it, now threaded with white fire, and began to feed it into the veil. At first, it longed to draw power from the network, and I understood the temptation Xeoniteridone felt, to feed from it and grow in power beyond anything anyone could ever imagine. But I wasn't him, and the thought continued to evolve into sickening disgust at the idea of destroying the Universe for my own gain.

Yes, Max sent, his people humming a song of agreement. *We, too, know the lure of such power. But, like us, you are now responsible for the safety of the veil, if only your corner of it.* He showed me the lines between planes. *You know what you must do?*

I didn't, not really, but my sorcery seemed to. Now subdued from its need to feed, I felt the draw on it, as it touched the old connections, the familiarity it expressed at the feeling of each plane.

Do I do it all at once? I braced myself for a massive output of power. While I was pretty sure it wouldn't do me permanent damage, I didn't know what kind of a state I'd be in when it was over. *Or one at a time?*

I believe, Max sent, *all together might be the best scenario. Just in case the Node seals itself and doesn't allow further additions.*

I felt hands on my physical body, a hard chest pressed to my shoulder and a whisper of my name in my ear. Comforted Ram was with me, at least where I could feel him, I allowed my sorcery to spread out and touch each and every one of the lost planes.

They spoke to me suddenly, as though alive, the power in them eager and willing to be brought back together. Like a long-parted family, they longed to be returned to their familiar state.

Now, Meira, Max sent. *Pull them together.*

I assumed it would be a strain, no matter the eagerness of the planes, and so, with a mighty heave, I threw everything I had into it.

Thank the elements for Max and the drach. The planes rushed toward each other like freight trains on collision courses, moving so easily I jerked them into reverse in an attempt not to cause an apocalypse in my attempt to make things right. The drach's magic steadied the influx of planes, sliding them together like pieces of a jigsaw puzzle.

You could have warned me. I was certain my hair stood on end on my physical body, I was so wound up.

I had no idea you would try to make them fit, Max sent with a hint of humor in his voice. *All is well.*

I nudged a few slowpoke planes to make them catch

up and watched in awe as the edges came together, dimming black, then glimmering white, and finally flaring bright gold a moment before they snapped into place and the entirety of Demonicon settled back to normal.

My power slammed back into my body, my knees wobbling slightly as I returned. Ram's gentle, supporting presence held me upright while I pressed one hand to my forehead and let out a shaky laugh, looking up to meet the drach leader's eyes.

"Well," I said. "That was fun."

His diamond gaze glittered as he pointed over my shoulder. "Nicely done, Ruler."

I turned, realized the entire throne room was quiet, and realized only then why everyone was staring. There, in the middle of the massive space, hovered the new Node, the tear-drop shape pulsing and swaying in the air over the polished stone floor. And above, the sky swelled with suns, returned to the familiar, beloved view I was used to.

Awe shone on every face, even the hardest and most jaded of my court, Henemordonin included. My grandfather remained on his knees, looking up at the Node with his hands clasped under his chin.

I could feel them even stronger now, I realized, each and every soul of demonkind linked to me, their thoughts and feelings tied to mine. It felt familiar, like being part of the coven again, though I knew, with time, this would fade. And had to. No way could I carry millions of minds with me all the time.

The brush of another, the whisper of power, jerked me forward toward the Node. I reached inside of it, and let out a choking laugh filled with tears.

Grandmother! She was there, woven into the fabric of the energy keeping our world together once and for all. And was it just me, or was the power of the Node less amber and more a pale gold?

It took her a moment to respond and when she did, her mind felt different.

Meira, she sent, sounding calm and distant.

I'm glad you're okay. Was she? Was she really?

I am, she sent, stronger, more herself, and shifting as we spoke. *I piggy-backed on Ostrogotho's power when the Node separated.* She sounded briefly confused. *I don't remember what happened after that. Until I woke up here.* Her magic touched mine, no longer her own, but a part of the Node and as inseparable as any of the planes. *Are you well? Is it over?*

It is, I sent, letting my power slide free of hers. *We won, Grandmother.*

That's nice, dear, she sent, distant again.

I hugged myself, worry and guilt rising all over again. Another arm embraced me as Syd joined me in front of the pulsing power source.

"She's fine," Syd said. "You did it, Meems."

"But Grandmother." What would happen to her?

"She is now a part of Demonicon," Max said softly over my sister's shoulder. "An integral part of what makes this world whole. Her power and soul will remain in the Node, influencing its development." I wondered what that meant. "And, knowing Ahbi Sanghamitra, she wouldn't want it any other way."

Syd laughed, arm tightening around me. "You got that right."

I found myself smiling, tears trickling down my face. "You know," I said, "I have to agree, too." I turned in Syd's embrace, Ram's arm still around my waist, and faced Max. "One left to find," I said.

He nodded, though the lack of concern he showed the last time I mentioned Mabel had slipped. So he was worried about her. Kind of him to keep it from me until I could do something about it.

"You were with her," he said. "You know the lack of anything existing in the void between planes."

"But she could still be okay, you said so before." She had to be.

He shrugged and then nodded with a sigh. "We can try," he said. "But I warn you, Meira. No creature who has gone to the void has ever been retrieved."

Syd gasped beside me. "You didn't think that was important to mention?"

"We had larger issues to handle," Max said, sadness

clear on his face now. "And Mabel would never want us to give up on doing what we needed to. She and I—and all drach—understand the necessity of sacrifice."

"That's a load of crap if ever I've heard it," Syd snapped. "Freaking idiot drach and your damned sense of responsibility." She turned her back on him and grabbed both of my hands. "Let's find her."

I was very grateful for the help, enough some more tears escaped. "Where do we start?"

A heavy weight landed on my feet. I looked down to see Sassafras staring up at me.

"She told you how," he said. "The bloodline, remember?"

Right. She was our ancestor. I nodded to Syd and opened my magic to her. Her eyes widened a little as she had a peek around, sampling the white sorcery with my permission.

"Nice," she said.

I knew my magic held nothing to what she had at her command. But I felt more powerful than I ever had and nodded. "Just something I threw together," I said. "Now, we need to identify what she feels like."

Both of us hunted through each other, looking for hints of Mabel. Sassafras found it before either of us, his sharp, "ah-ha!" in our heads making me roll my eyes and smile down at him.

"I don't remember inviting you to the party," Syd

said.

"You two couldn't find yourselves in a dark room," he sniffed. "Here. This is Mabel."

He showed me, made me feel her, far below my power, deeper than my soul, from the very depths of who I was. The hint of the drach. And there, in Syd, the same feeling. It grew stronger, rising from my very bones, from the marrow of them, from the casings of my cells to coalesce like a beacon, growing stronger as I focused on it.

Syd nodded sharply to me. "Okay," she said. "Got her scent. Let's do this thing."

I stepped back from Ram, from Sassafras who curled his tail around his paws and watched us go. Max tore a gap in the veil and leaped through. I followed my sister, hand in hand, landing behind her on Max's broad back as he soared in the darkness. But the view I'd gained when I reassembled the Node hadn't left me, and it was only a moment before my eyes adjusted and I could see the lines between planes.

Would she still be between Bilhaeder and the other plane? That might make things complicated. I couldn't very well break up the Node again to rescue Mabel. And yet, I was perfectly willing to try.

No, Max sent. *The void, like the veil, is everywhere. If she is still reachable, we should be able to find her at any juncture.* He didn't sound completely convinced of his own explanation, but it was all I had to cling to.

He banked, carrying us forward to hover over a separation line in the veil.

This is the place where your world, Syd, he showed us Wilding Springs, *meets Demonicon*. I could feel it, the familiarity of it, and wondered why he brought us here. *Because you both know this section of the veil so well, it may be our best hope at creating a pocket of the void.*

Will this damage the veil any more than it already is? Though Xeoniteridone's plan failed, I knew the hurt to the protective barrier between Universes couldn't take much more before we were in serious trouble.

It shouldn't. Again, Max sounded reluctantly optimistic. *There is only one way to discover the truth, however.*

Syd's power hummed, ready and willing. *No more talking it over*, she sent. *My husband and kids are waiting on supper.*

No matter how bad or dangerous the situation, she always managed to make me laugh.

In the end, it was much simpler than any of us expected. With Syd's magic on one side and mine on the other, pulling an edge apart wasn't all that difficult. Max then inserted his own like a wedge, holding the space open. The empty void gaped beneath us, complete darkness the black of my sorcery, woven with the new clean white I acquired from Xeoniteridone. The void seemed to react to the pale flames, recoiling slightly as though this were some foreign and unwelcome magic it couldn't tolerate. With my melding of old and new sorcery, tied to Syd's and fed into the bloodline connection we had with Mabel, I called to the lost drach.

There was no answer at first, only a deathly silence that broke my heart. I called and reached and fought to find her, certain at any moment she would appear out of the black, wings flapping. Nothing. Not a trace or a breath of Mabel.

We can't do this forever, Syd sent. *I'm sorry, Meems.*

Just another moment, I sent. *Please. I know she's there.*

She is, Max sent with a keen edge of sorrow, *but it's possible she's long lost to us, now a part of the void herself.*

I refused to betray her by quitting too soon. But even I had to admit, long moments—and maybe hours for all I knew in the quiet of the veil—there was simply nothing there to find.

All right, I finally eased up, heart breaking for her loss. *You two win.*

Syd's magic hugged me. *I'm sorry, Meems. It's not right, but sometimes we just have to accept the crappy stuff with the good.*

Could I just let go and allow Mabel to be lost forever? I am ashamed I was about to when, for a bright and shining moment, I felt her. The briefest touch, just a brushing of consciousness. It was enough I threw myself toward her with renewed hope, Syd right beside me, our pulses beating in rapid time together as hope lived at last.

Syd and I tied our magic tightly together and sent it tumbling into the gap, morphing into a spear of magic now driving forward, everywhere and yet nowhere at once. A glimmer of life beckoned, the faintest breath of a mind, but it was Mabel and we both knew her the moment we found her.

The spear turned to a net, slipping around her drach form. I heaved when she was inside, Syd straining with me as Max trembled beneath us. I could feel the wedge slipping as all of our focus shifted to lifting Mabel out of nothing and into the veil, leaving the drach leader to take up the slack of keeping the void space open. It was as though our power had no juice in the dark, our strength drops of water on a vast forest fire.

The drach joined us in a rush, wings flapping, coming to hover around us in a singing circle. The veil filled with the sound of their song, the wedge strengthening, their power joining ours in pulling Mabel to freedom.

The white flames of my new sorcery burned a hole in the darkness, lending strength to Syd and me, cutting through the black like a shining sword of light. Strength renewed, Syd and I heaved with all our power, the net pulled tight as though the void refused to give Mabel back to us. But this was a fight I would not lose.

When she finally cleared the void, I sobbed into the dark at the sight of her, white flames flickering around her limp form. Pale, almost translucent, her wings furled

218

around her, diamond eyes empty, she sagged lifelessly against the woven blanket of our supporting power. But when Max and the others let the void slip shut, Mabel stirred, weakly lifted her head, and met my gaze.

Thank you, she whispered, barely audible. *I knew you would come for me.*

I cried as the drach took her from us and carried her through a gap in the veil and out of my sight.

CHAPTER TWENTY FOUR

I stood at the railing of the balcony, looking out over my favorite view. Ostrogotho stretched out beneath me, the repairs mostly completed, the cluster of suns overhead shining down on the black stone city. New rock had just arrived from the mines at Bilhaeder. I'd had a brief conversation with Questorin, the new supervisor of the mining operation there. He seemed to be taking his responsibilities very seriously, a fact that made me both happy and almost giggly.

"It was the sorcery's drain creating the brittleness in the rock," he said when I called to check up on him, covered in rock dust, but his young face eager and earnest. "Everything seems to have gone back to normal."

That was good to know.

"You'll have what you need within the day," he

finished our conversation. "With our thanks, my Ruler."

I said goodbye to the loyal young miner and tried to ignore the look of worship in his eyes. Partly because that particular expression was more common than not lately and I wasn't sure I was ready to be put on that kind of a pedestal.

"You saved them all from a horrible fate," Syd said with a grin when I brought it up last night over a private dinner. She looked much more relaxed and calm, not nearly as tired. "Expect a little hero worship for a while. At least until they start bickering among themselves again."

I smiled it off, though I was beginning to wonder if something fundamental had changed in my people. There had been reports of demons helping demons rebuild their homes without requesting compensation, random acts of kindness and valor. My hands tightened on the ledge as I thought about it.

A kinder, gentler demon race. What a novelty.

They weren't the only ones who had changed. Now that I'd had a few days to rest without a crisis looming to keep me on my toes, exploration of my new power yielded some interesting discoveries. I felt calm, the calmest I ever had, and older, almost. Matured, maybe, was a better word. Part of me chalked it up to the full support—still ongoing—of the demon populace. Though I had been right about my connection to them fading with time, I could still feel them as a collective, like a second heartbeat inside me.

But ultimately, I knew it came from the clean, white sorcery I was only beginning to understand. Sorcery I sensed in every one of my subjects and the Node itself.

My gaze drifted down to the Parade and the bustle of activity there. I snorted a little, hand over my mouth, still finding it amusing a giant statue was being erected in the massive space. A statue of me. Embarrassment at the idea turned me from the ledge and sent me inside my quarters where I could forget for a moment.

Of course, seeing the growing statue only reminded me of the rumors circulating. Sequoia had gleefully informed me only yesterday songs were being written about my valor and the defeat of Xeoniteridone.

It wouldn't have been so bad if Sassafras hadn't poked his nose in. "How quaint," he said, swiping one paw with his tongue. "Don't let it go to your head."

I paced my quarters, mind turning. A certain measure of restlessness had taken me over the last day or so. I'd been on constant alert and under imminent threat for so long, having nothing to do seemed fundamentally wrong somehow. With the unanimous decision of the court, I was firmly back on First Seat. But Second Seat was glaringly empty, my grandfather now gone.

Not dead, though. I'd planned to kill him, I really had. But when they brought him before me, a broken shell of who he'd been, I didn't have the heart. Instead, I drained his power almost completely dry, leaving him enough to retain his mind, and set him up in the care of the Daeva, now with the learning level of a child and the innocence that went with it.

It was odd to stand in the threshold of a brightly lit room overlooking the ocean, watching my grandfather giggle and play with one of his nannies as though he were only a small boy.

"You did a kind turn for him," Raethnn told me. "Any other Ruler would have had him killed no matter his turn of heart."

Any other Ruler. I'd left the Daeva leader and my fallen grandfather with a heavy heart, thinking of another lost to me. I'd tried to reach Ahbi a few times, but without success. After transporting the Node to its chamber, I'd done my best to reconnect with my grandmother. But whether she was fully absorbed now, or simply unwilling to talk to me, I didn't know.

At least she was alive and well—as far as I knew—inside the Node. Why, then, did I miss her like a hole in my heart?

I sat on the edge of a chair and leaned back, closing my eyes. Dinner last night had been informative, Syd telling me the damage to the veil was finally reversing. Max was very pleased with the results and the drach expected full recovery within the week. The only trouble was what had come through during the damage.

"We'll have some fun cleaning up the mess," she said with a wink, "but it's nothing we can't handle."

I hoped she was right. Then again, a little crisis might be fun right about now.

Did I really call trouble fun? Oh dear. Syd was really rubbing off on me.

The best part about dinner? My sister hugging me before she left, whispering in my ear.

"I'm so proud of you."

For the first time, we were equals. All resentment toward her fled at last as I hugged her back.

When Sassafras interrupted us, I bent to scoop him into my arms, kissing his soft forehead.

"I'm happy to stay," he said, looking to Syd for agreement. She nodded, though she seemed sad. "If you need me."

I hugged him, too, and handed him to my sister with a smile. "Thank you," I said. "But you have two Hayle children to watch over. This one is doing just fine."

He wiped his paw over his nose. "You don't need me anymore." So soft, so sad.

I laughed and kissed him again, then my sister. "Silly cat," I said. "I'll always need you. But they need you more."

Bittersweet, when Syd stepped through the veil, Sass in her arms. And yet, when the gash closed, I breathed a soft sigh of contentment.

Maybe he was right, and I was just being kind. Regardless, knowing the people I loved were there for me no matter what made all the difference.

The restlessness finally got the better of me. I stood and strode from the room, heading for the secret passage and the staircase. I'd taken to using it to move around the Seat, though I'd made veil travel legal for those who could achieve it. Turned out it was a lost art, but one many demons were relearning, thanks to the return of their sorcery.

The antidote hadn't stripped them of their ability to use it, turned out. Instead, like me, the demon race now had access to both. And while I was waiting for the shoe to drop, for the monsters in them to finally rise, knowing how balanced I felt being whole made me wonder if the reappearance of sorcery on Demonicon was actually a very good thing. Fear had a way of making those in power want to diminish those below them, and I knew there was a time when having sorcery meant a threat to the safety and well-being of my people. That didn't seem to be the case anymore. And this new kind of sorcery seemed to be the cause.

I couldn't wait to see what that meant for all of us.

My feet tapped on the steps, down three levels to the lab. I slipped through the gap in the rock and down the narrow corridor, through the sliding door and into the main laboratory. A smile pulled at my mouth as I spotted Theridialis and Portlish hunched over a large book, a row of multi-colored liquids bubbling before them.

The two had become fast friends, and though Theridialis had as yet to recover fully, he looked much better and actually more youthful without all his extra weight. Portlish even seemed altered, though his hero worship wasn't aimed at me, by any means. He reserved all of it for his mentor.

Sequoia smiled and waved from the corner where she perched, reading on a low stool. I joined her rather than disturb the eager pair who whispered between each other like giddy kids trying something they probably shouldn't.

"Nice to see your father up and about," I said as Sequoia set her book aside to hug me.

"It is," she said, beaming in his direction. "I've never seen him so enthusiastic."

I sank down on the stool next to her. "What are they working on?"

Sequoia laughed and shook her head. "Who knows? It's beyond me." She patted my hand. "That was a wonderful thing you did for Portlish."

I shrugged and folded my hands in my lap. "As if I'd let Frestendel have him back." The nectar dealer had come to me shortly after the restoration, looking for his payment. I'd agreed to give him anything he wanted if Portlish was successful. While the cook tried to insist it wasn't him, his old boss insisted.

"You promised," he held his ground despite Jabuticabron's fury. "And I expect you to fulfil that promise, Ruler."

"So I shall." I nodded. "Ask for your anything."

The list was long and grew grandly as his recitation went on. By the time he was asking for full access to the Node, I shut him down.

"Anything," I said. "Means one thing."

Frestendel tried to argue, but finally agreed on a higher plane elevation and enough riches to keep him happy for however long he lived.

"It will do," he sniffed at me before turning and gesturing at Portlish. "Come, time to go."

The cook didn't budge, mostly because I held him back with magic.

"Didn't I tell you?" I smiled at the dealer as he spun on me in fury. "Because of his contribution, I've elevated Portlish to a Duke of the Third plane." Which, it turned out, was about ten planes above Frestendel. "He only answers to his Ruler, now."

The dealer spluttered and the dealer argued. But, in the end, under threat of having his request reversed, Frestendel left.

"Portlish is meant for more than cooking nectar," I said to Sequoia, rising from my seat, ready to move on again. This restlessness made me uncomfortable.

"Agreed," my friend said. She reached for my hand, a little frown between her brows. "Are you well, Meira?"

I nodded, squeezed her fingers, and let them drop. "Fine," I said. "Just checking in." I left her there, not bothering to interrupt the excited pair of scientists, heading up toward the throne room by the back elevator. I stared out over the ocean below, lost in its glittering expanse, remaining there even after the platform came to a halt.

"My Ruler." I turned at the sound of Jabuticabron's voice. He waited patiently for me at the edge of the elevator, offering his hand for stability as I crossed to the polished floor. "You asked to be informed when she was brought in."

She. My darling cousin, Tanasharia. "You've captured her?"

"She's in your office right now," he said, satisfaction in his graveled voice.

Most excellent. I turned and stepped onto the elevator again, my guard captain beside me as we dropped a level. "Let's put an end to this despicable branch of the family, once and for all."

chapter twenty five

Rutorith stood at attention outside my office door. When I approached, he straightened himself further, one good eye staring straight ahead, face grim. I paused next to him and nodded for him to relax his stance.

"Is your new appointment to your liking?" Despite his actions against me, I was well aware the old soldier was only doing what he thought was right. And such loyalty, even if poorly placed, wasn't to be squandered.

He bowed his head to me, iron gray hair cropped close to his scarred skull. "It is, my Ruler," he said, same harsh voice untouched by emotion, though I could see a hint of regret in his lined and time-beaten face. "My gratitude for your understanding and kindness, my Ruler."

I waved his words off. "You serve me half as well as you did my grandfather," I said, moving on through the open doors to my office, "and it will have been worth it."

There was little doubt in my mind I'd ever have trouble from him again.

Old anger bubbled in my gut as I strode down the steps and across the room to my massive desk. Two guards held Tanasharia, bound with heavy metal cuffs on wrists and ankles, waiting for me. Images and memories of her despicable father, Vandelarius, Ahbi's Second Seat and her vile brother, Cypherion, long stripped by my sister, churned my stomach acid until I swallowed bile.

A bad fruit not fallen far from her family tree, Tanasharia's defiance and hatred shone through for the briefest moment before she fell to her knees at my feet and pretended to blubber. She was, in fact, an excellent blubberer, but despite the enjoyment I took from her state, I had better things to do with my time.

"Get up." My words slashed her like knives. Her false sobs ended, head coming up, amber eyes reflecting her hate once more. Jabut moved forward, grasping her by her shoulder and bodily pulling her to her feet. I prodded her with power, feeling her mix of sorcery and demon magic hiss spitefully back.

"Ruler," she gushed the words, sickly-sweet sincerity just making my insides twist further. "I beg you, forgive me." She licked her dry lower lip, eyes darting sideways to Jabut. "I was coerced, only following orders I was forced to obey—"

"Correct me if I'm wrong, Jabuticabron," I cut her off with casual deliberation. "But the demons we captured who were among Xeoniteridone's elite. They weren't possessed by coercion, nor did the nectar they drank mimic the effects of the one he used on the populace."

"You are absolutely right, my Ruler," he said, anger surfacing in his voice. "We discovered the cult leader hand selected a number of demons to follow him who were permitted to keep their demon power and serve him without coercion. Tanasharia was one of them."

I knew that already, but it was nice to watch her squirm. Part of me chided myself for being so silly, suggested I simply strip her and send her to her death without all the theatrics. But she felt, to me, like the last thread of a long and torrid story, and I wanted to deal with her personally.

She was family, after all. It was the very least I could do.

Meira, Sequoia's mental voice reached through my need to punish my cousin as my diminutive friend entered my office. She came in quietly, as she always did, but the tone of her voice finally broke the hold my need to crush Tanasharia had over me.

I waved at Jabut, turning my back. "Have her stripped," I said, no longer caring. "Do it yourself, as a reward." I didn't want her power inside me, all of a sudden, and hers would serve my guard captain very well.

Tanasharia squealed her fury, but Jabut spoke over her.

"My thanks, Ruler," he said. I listened to her struggle, the clank of her bonds as he dragged her away. And the final, vile screeching as he hauled her out the door.

Sequoia's little hand settled over mine. "It was a kind gift you gave my brother." She sighed. "I'm sorry, Meira."

"I'm not." I shivered, rubbed my arms with both hands, turning to smile down at her. "It's over now. I can move on and rebuild my court without worry about the family." They had, as yet, to discover my plans for the reshuffle. But I wasn't about to let them in on the process until I had sufficient guards present to control them when they freaked out. From now on, presence in court would be held by merit, not by blood.

Things would be interesting for a while. I couldn't wait to see what Demonicon's ruling class looked like when the dust finally settled.

"You were also kind to spare those who worked against you on your grandfather's behalf." She sounded like she disapproved this time.

"They have theirs coming, remember?" His shadow court was in for the biggest fall of all. Those who didn't help him, just participated in the usual backstabbing, would at least keep their riches and some of their property. But those who joined Henemordonin willingly?

They were in for a rude wake up call. Very shortly,

they would not only be stripped of their homes, their wealth would be seized and distributed to the new ruling class.

I couldn't wait.

The air beside me sighed, a gash opening as a tall, black-haired drach stepped through. She was still pale, her skin a bit sunken, powerful body thin to the point I still saw hard edged bone through her flesh. But the sparkle in Mabel's diamond eyes told me she was in good humor as she bowed her head to me, long hair sweeping over the floor.

"Meira," she said.

"Nana." I grinned up at her. "How are you feeling?" Max had been kind enough to take me to her bedside a few days ago so I could reassure myself she was all right. She didn't wake from her unconscious state, but her mind was strong and her power rebuilding so I knew she would recover.

"I am well," she said. "Weary from my battle against the void. But your rescue has ensured my continued existence and, for that, I will always be grateful."

I hugged her impulsively, hearing her heartbeat under my ear as she embraced me back.

"Since you created me, ultimately," I said into her chest, "we're even."

She smiled down at me as I leaned away, touching my hair with one hand, hesitant, as though unsure if such a gesture was welcome or not. "Agreed," she said.

I stepped away from her, holding one of her hands. It felt wonderful to have her with me again. I missed Ahbi so much, having Mabel back in my life was a massive relief. "You're not helping with the repairs to the veil?" I almost kicked myself for blurting those words. She had to be too weak to help, and I was sure that would bother her.

Instead, she shrugged. "I chose to return to you," she said. "And Max agreed. This is my place, now. In fact," she squeezed my fingers, "he is now considering placing drach with other key power figures around the veil, to prevent occurrences like this one from getting ahead of us."

Well, that was a revelation. "He just agreed because he knew I wouldn't give you back."

Her laughter was the song of the drach. "Perhaps you're right." She released my hand, folding hers in front of her. "Part of my task will be training you to use your sorcery to your best benefit."

I felt it coiling inside me, still hungry, always hungry, though the black at times warred with the white over such need. My people were forever changed by it, the mingling of both sorceries as much a part of them now—and our new Node—as it was of me. Up to this point, I'd done fine under pressure, figuring things out as I went along. But being ahead of the curve for once, knowing how to guide my fellow demons in this new power as well as day-to-day rule? I really needed to step up from here on it. Besides, it would be nice to have a little more experience under the watchful eye of my drach friend.

For the first time since this all started, I actually felt happy. I turned to the door, thinking the exercise gym a few levels below would be a good spot for working with her, thanks to all the shielding, when the air beside me rippled again. But this time, there was no veil tear. Just the golden shape of a demon I knew very well.

I cried out, hands covering my mouth, tears in my eyes as Ahbi Sanghamitra materialized before me, smiling. She looked young, so much younger than the demon Ruler I'd come to know, closer to my age in appearance. I saw myself in her, Syd, Dad even, soaking in her new look as she spoke.

"Sorry to be so absent." She held out her glowing amber hands with a smile on her face. "I've been adjusting to my new home."

Mabel bowed to her. "It is good to see you well, Ahbi."

"And you," she said. "I'm glad the girls were able to pull you out of the void."

"Grandmother." I choked out the word.

"My dear Meira," she said with a laugh. "Don't look so upset. I'm fine, I really am. But I do have a warning for you."

My hackles rose instantly, fear biting through my anxiety for her. "What's wrong?"

Again her laugh, the toss of her head, amber fire hair rippling. "Nothing's specifically wrong," she said. "But you should know I'm now a permanent part of the Node."

I nodded, relaxing a little. "I already knew that. Max told me."

She shook her head, fire passing over her glowing eyes. "I don't think you get it," she said. "Remember the conversation we had about how your sister and I changed the Node through our interaction with it?"

I did, vaguely. "So?"

She reached out with her phantom hand and touched the tip of my nose with one finger. "I was born into this new Node," she said, full of mischief. "With control over the fabulous white sorcery that seems to have developed out of this mess. So expect the unexpected, won't you?"

"Grandmother." I gaped at her. "What did you do?"

"Nothing." Her innocence was clearly faked. "Just making some adjustments to the way things work around here. Hope you don't mind."

I flapped my lips like a landed fish, unable to speak as she leaned in and kissed my cheek.

"Don't worry," she whispered in my ear as she faded out of sight. *I have been and always will be on your side. Let's make Demonicon a world to be proud of.*

That I could buy into. And yet, why did her meddling make me nervous? Because she was my grandmother, that's why.

Now I really needed something to distract me. I turned to Mabel and gestured toward the door with a slight wince.

"I think learning to use my sorcery is an excellent idea," I said. "I have a feeling, with Grandmother poking around in the Node and making changes, I'm going to need it sooner than later."

ChAPTER TWENTY SIX

My throne was uncomfortable as usual, but this time I didn't notice so much. Victory had a way of softening even the hard stone of the seat beneath me and after sparring with Mabel for a few hours, I didn't have the power to waste on cushioning my backside.

Just a few more details to hammer out before the real work began. Part of that work stood before me in open view in front of the badly shaken and now fearful court. They had so much more to look forward to. I couldn't wait. But, for now, it was immensely satisfying to see the overdressed and formerly pompous crowd of family shaking in their fur and elaborate costumes as the Daeva lined the center aisle in their vast numbers.

They even gave me the creeps, so I could only imagine how my family felt.

"Ruler." Raethnn bowed to me, "it is with great pride

and respect we welcome you home to your throne. And long may you hold the power of Demonicon in your possession." She didn't have to glare at the gathering. Rumors of who they were and why they'd come had spread quickly. Having spent most of my childhood in the coven, I had no idea the Daeva was long whispered about and feared, the proverbial boogeydemons come to life enough to keep the family silent and still.

"And First Seat offers you our deepest thanks, Mistress Raethnn," I said, "for your timely assistance in helping rebuild our world."

Again she bowed. "We would no longer hide in the shadows." I didn't want her to, so I was okay with that. "The Daeva would be your personal guard, Ruler, at your side at all times." While I didn't think I needed them in that capacity, it would be nice, to be honest, having unwaveringly loyal demons to count on in the next little while when the court shuffle took place. So I nodded. "We have one final request, and it is a request." Her amber eyes glittered, but with amusement or intensity, I couldn't say. "As a show of faith, we would offer one of our own as Second Seat."

I choked, coughing, spluttering. It took me a moment to pull myself under some kind of control as Rameranselot stepped out from behind the group of Daeva and joined Raethnn. His face was blank, but his head high and I wondered if she'd pressured him into this.

"We offer one of our most beloved sons," Raethnn said, lined hand falling on his shoulder. "Rameranselot will serve you well, not only as Second Seat, but as your mate, if you so choose."

More choking. "You know the law," I said when I could speak, not looking at Ram, so confused and stirred up inside I needed to stall. "Only the most powerful can sit on the Second Seat of Demonicon."

Ram stiffened next to Raethnn as she spoke. "I think you will find he can defeat any demon here with the audacity to challenge him." Not a single voice spoke up in protest. In fact, I'm certain I could have heard a snowflake fall in the utter silence following her words.

Trouble was, my anger had finally taken over. I glared down at Raethnn, tired of the bullying and the posturing. I'd come through the other side of that, thank you, and had no interest in perpetuating it. Yes, I was about to unleash my own slice of hell on the court once I had all my pieces in place, but I would not be intimidated or have a relationship like this one shoved down my throat.

"Denied," I said.

Ram's look of hurt was so fast, flashing over his face, I almost felt guilty. Almost. Damn him, he'd turned me down over and over, citing his lowly plane level and the fact his life was complicated. Well, now I knew the truth, didn't I? He lied about being able to claim Second Seat, clearly. And it seemed the Daeva were more than willing to allow those other "complications" to fall to the wayside.

I would not be controlled ever again, not even for Ram. So I ignored his slightly sagging shoulders and the growing scowl on Raethnn's face.

"I am Ruler here," I said, letting my voice boom with a push of power. "And I decide who takes Second Seat. And whom I choose for my mate. Not you, Daeva." *And don't forget it,* I sent directly to her.

We thought this was what you wanted, Raethnn sent, not exactly contrite, but not all that harsh about it, either. *I'm sorry if we were wrong.*

I need to make my own choices from here on in, I sent, softer this time. *If our people are finally going to evolve, we need new rules, new ways of being. And I won't allow myself to stray from the path I've chosen, not even for my own personal happiness.*

Raethnn bowed her head one last time. "As you wish, Ruler," she said and backed off.

Taking Rameranselot with her. Damn it, I had to do something about him, I guessed. But the school-girl crush I had on him had burned away in the trials of the last few weeks. Did I even really love him? I barely knew him.

You know him, Mabel sent as the Daeva filed away in perfect symmetry. *And you know your heart. He completes you.*

That's nice, I sent, a little more sharply than I intended. *Maybe if he asked instead of making it an ultimatum.*

I have a feeling, she sent, *this wasn't his choice to make.*

Exactly my point. I sat back on my throne as the court finally relaxed slightly, still looking nervously around. *I'm done doing what's expected. We all are. Time to roust the house and drag demonkind into the light.*

Mabel's mind hugged mine. *I knew you were the perfect choice,* she sent. *Now, put an end to this farce of a session and let us return to our training.*

I groaned. Out loud. But I did as I was told. I guess there was still one person who could boss me around.

I sank into a chair in my quarters, my whole body aching and my sorcery complaining loudly it was starving, that I'd worked it too hard and where was the power it needed to replenish itself?

Thankfully my other magicks were there to siphon energy into it, the pulse of the power of Demonicon giving the most. I worried such an arrangement might weaken me, but according to Mabel, I was simply creating a circle of consumption that was actually the best way to keep my sorcery in check.

So she said. I could only trust and believe in her. She'd finally let me go after a few hours of training and I'd only now staggered my way back to my room to try to recover from the beating she'd delivered. Not literally, but she'd worked me so hard I expected to have bruises.

The last thing I wanted was to move, but a hot bath

was the only thing I could think of to make me feel better.

"Pagomaris." My voice croaked as I called her name. She didn't appear and only then did I remember my faithful aide was gone, back with the Daeva. She'd tearfully confessed she couldn't stay with me any longer. Her years with Ahbi and then with me had blunted her abilities and, by choice, she returned to her people to hone her training.

It hurt, feeling like abandonment. But I'd find another aide.

Since I had, as yet, to do so, I was forced to take care of things myself. So funny, really. I was more powerful than ever, and here I was without the help I needed to run me a simple bath. Well, I was just Meira once—still was, as far as I was concerned—and Senne Hathenemeria, First Seat and Ruler of Demonicon, was not above turning some damned taps.

Come to think of it, I could probably have handled the whole situation with some magic, but the idea of using my power just now made me groan. At this rate, Xeoniteridone and his followers could have left me be. Mabel was going to succeed in killing me herself.

My bathroom was dark, the lighting coming on low when I passed my hand over the crystal on the wall, triggering the magic of the Seat to flood the soft lights with illumination. I bent over the massive tub, the golden faucets gleaming in the low light, when I realized I wasn't alone.

I turned with a gasp, power ready, aches forgotten, ready to cut down whoever faced me.

Only to drop my control and sag a little at the sight of Ram's angry face.

"Hi," I said, voice barely above a whisper. Facing off with him in the throne room, surrounded by demons and being pressured to marry him was one thing. My own temper had taken over, and fair enough. But seeing him here, in person, woke the feelings I had for him with a vengeance, so much I knew Mabel was right. I did love him after all, despite everything.

But from the fury in his eyes, I'd done more damage than I might be able to repair by rejecting him publicly.

The water flowed, steam pouring up from the taps, as he spoke, voice trembling.

"I thought this was what you wanted." His hands shook as he ran them both through his hair before falling deathly still. "You made it clear you wanted to be with me."

"I did," I said. "I do."

"You have a funny way of showing it." His cheeks darkened as he looked away. "Do you have any idea how much it took for me to stand there and have Raethnn offer me up like some prize you'd won?" His voice shook with emotion. "I've spent my life following the orders of my leader, being used and manipulated. By Raethnn and by Ahbi." He took a step back, hands clenching at his sides. "Well, just so you know, I'm done with being told what to do, too, no matter how I feel about you." Passion vibrated in his every word.

"Good," I said.

His teeth squeaked as he ground them together. "I don't think you understand," he growled. "I won't be sold, Meira. Not to you. Not for anything. And if you ever treat me that way again, I'll never forgive you."

"You're an idiot." I could have returned his anger, but I was through with fighting. My words weren't razored or fired with temper. They just were.

Ram took offense, as I knew he would. "Damn you," he cried. "Damn this whole plane and your Second Seat."

I took a step toward him, heart aching suddenly. "We've both been forced into too much," I said. "I understand. Ram, of anyone, I understand." I let that sink in as his anger faded and his shoulders sagged. "I know you don't love me. And that being with me was just part of your orders." He looked up sharply, face unreadable. "It's okay. I wanted to give you an out. I'm sorry it was so public." I really was. I wished Raethnn hadn't chosen to make me reject him in front of everyone, but she gave me no options. "You're free to do whatever you want. I refuse to be just another obligation. And I would hate you forever, Ram, if that was all I was to you."

"Thanks." His voice flattened out. "The public humiliation after you and my grandmother conspired to trap me really earned my trust."

"I swear," I said, keeping my own tone level, now just wanting to smack him for being a jerk, "I had no idea what she had in mind." I turned my back on him. "Had I, I would have said no right away. You've made it clear you have no interest in me, aside from maybe friendship." What about our exchange in the Daeva stronghold? I refused to cling to that. We were both looking for comfort in a time of crisis. I wouldn't hold him to anything he said or did, despite my feelings for him. It would hurt me to let him go, but the thought of a loveless and bitter mating, paired with a sullen Second Seat if he took the throne, just made me sick to my stomach.

Ram's head came up, defiance in his face. "Who says I don't have interest in you?"

Now I was really going to hit him. "You are the most contrary, stubborn, irritating—"

He barked a laugh, cutting me off. "I am?" His hands tossed in the air. "I finally thought we had a chance, that you'd grown up and could finally take what I had to offer seriously. But I guess I was wrong. You don't love me. You never did."

This about face had me reeling. "I'm sorry?" What the hell was he talking about?

Ram seemed confused himself, though more sad. "I

didn't want it to happen this way," he said. "Meira, I've loved you since I met you the first time." He... he what? "Even though you were so young, so innocent. Full of life and enthusiasm I'd never encountered in a demon before." Wonder briefly lit his eyes. "Your focus wasn't taking power, but understanding it. Do you have any idea how baffling that was to me?" He didn't pause to give me time to answer. "Syd told me to watch over you, but she didn't have to. There was no way, after our first meeting, I would ever let you out of my sight."

I gaped at him as the steam engulfed us.

"Why do you think I went after the Planeless?" Desperation colored his tone, his entire body as he stood rigid before me. "To save you, to protect you. I couldn't let anything happen to you. And since I had no control over the torture Henemordonin put you through, I saw this as a chance to act."

I shook my head. "I'll say it again," I whispered. "You're an idiot."

He flashed a little smile, tension easing. "I would have killed your grandfather myself if Raethnn hadn't forbid me to interfere."

"That's sweet," I said. And giggled. Only a demon would think murder was sweet.

Ram laughed, too, before sighing out a huge breath. "We're both idiots," he said.

"I beg to differ." I waved off my words. "I was

stupid," I said. "And needy and I don't blame you for holding me at arm's length."

"That was the last thing I wanted. But in the beginning, I couldn't be sure your feelings were anything more than your need to have someone to cling to. Meira, I wanted more than that." Ram's intensity had shifted, from anger to a hunger I recognized. But I wouldn't fall into this so easily, not after all I'd been through.

"You've lied to me," I said, "deceived me, and turned me away so many times I can't just believe you all of a sudden." My heart rejected my words, but I wasn't listening. "It's going to take a lot more than one sexy smile," and it was sexy, my goodness, yum, "to change anything."

Ram nodded. "I know," he said. "I have no right to be angry with you, Meira." He hesitated before shrugging. "This isn't how I wanted things to end."

More silence as we both pondered where this conversation was going.

Ram suddenly circled the tub, coming to my side. His lower lip trembled as his eyes locked on mine, brimming with tears. "I love you," he said. "No matter what that means to you now, if you care, or if you want me to go away forever. But I want you to know my feelings for you started long before you became Ruler. I'm not being forced into anything."

Grief choked me. I thought of all the times he had

been there for me and knew he was right to wait until I grew up. "I love you, too." I sobbed once. "I always have. And not because I need you, but because I want you for you. Not Rameranselot of the Daeva. Just my Ram."

He cupped my face in his hands before bending slowly toward me, as though to give me the chance to stop him. I didn't try, leaning toward him as he kissed me. The fire between us broke wide open, further than it ever had, and I was left gasping when he pulled away.

"Stay with me." I'd come through to the other side of my own pains and sorrows and discovered he was exactly who I wanted with me. My magic held him, gently, without force, but with longing so powerful it hurt. "I can do this alone," I whispered. "I know I can. But I don't want to." My vision swam with my own tears as I looked up at him again and saw the shock on his face. "I want you." I took a deep breath. "I can handle whatever comes." I could, too. "And as much as I'd like for that to be my only consideration, I can't lie to you. To have you beside me, knowing I could trust you unconditionally, like no other, you'd be perfect for Second Seat. For Demonicon." I paused, worried my next words would drive him away, but needing to say them. "But I need you for my heart and my soul and to complete me. Power be damned, Ram. I need you for me."

I stared as he stepped back.

"I never want this to be about duty for either of us,"

he said. "To end up despising each other a century from now, but not knowing how to let each other go. It still might end that way." I highly doubted it and, from the little smile he shared, so did he. "But at least we're both going into it of our own free will." He hesitated. "Aren't we?"

I nodded quickly, wiping at the tears on my face. "Absolutely."

He took my hands in his. "Then my answer is yes."

And finally, all the pieces of my world fell into place. A peace I never knew stole over my weary heart as Ram wrapped me in his arms, his lips once more taking possession of what had really been his all along.

I couldn't help but smile when we finally parted, our foreheads touching. Ram's grin grew, then altered as he bent to turn off the water. I watched as he slipped out of his shirt, the muscles of his bare chest bunching as he tossed it away. When he met my eyes, one of his brows arched upward, a sensuous smile now pulling at the corner of his mouth.

"The water looks perfect," he said, reaching for me. "But we need to test it to find out."

It wasn't long before we found out just how perfect.

Like what you read? Find out more at
pattilarsen.com

Don't despair! There's more from the
Hayle Coven Universe ahead!

Here's a look at the first chapter of
Book One of Charlotte's trilogy,
The Lychos Cycle

WEREGIRL

ONE

My paws don't even seem to touch the ground as I bound and race through the quiet forest. Muscles bunch and pull, the remains of my human form slowing me only slightly as I stretch out my gait and push myself to top speed. My front paws reach and pull at the trees to propel me forward as my curved back legs churn faster.

There are times I wish wearing the true form of a wolf wouldn't steal my soul. Still, this hybrid human/beast shape has always served me well. Though I've laughed at Hollywood's attempt to recreate us for film, I have to admit they are very close to getting it right.

Wind stings my eyes, trees whipping past. My claws rend gashes in the bark of an evergreen as I use it to alter course, the sling shot effect pushing me faster. Three bounds and I come to rest on a rotting stump, crouching, muzzle hanging open, tongue lolling to the side as I grin into the still air and wait for the return of night time birdsong.

It doesn't take the local owls long to forgive my trespass, the who-who-who of their quiet communication perking my ears, so deep and beautiful to my wolf ears. The scent of dying vegetation mixed with the soft breath of coming fall filters through my sensitive nose, a winding pattern of scents carrying on the breeze. Prey animals, small and quick, poke their own noses out from under dying leaves before scurrying off to hide, not understanding I am not a threat.

Moonlight filters through the towering branches, more than enough to illuminate my path. I hold my place as a grumpy wolverine snuffles his way past, out of respect for his touchy nature as much as my amusement at the way his round body, fattening for winter, waddles by.

I love the forest, the ancient touch of it. I feel the most free here, unchained by titles and my grandfather's constant prodding. Fall is coming to Ukraine, another year winding into the next and I have, as of yet, to satisfy his need for an heir of my own to the throne of the werenation.

A delicate shudder ruffles my fur as I think of my friends, Syd and Meira. I'm not the only one who has faced these demands to mate, to make more of me for the continuation of my line. My witch friends endured their own torments before finding their true love. I've felt the culmination of their desires in them both. Smelled it, the sweet and subtle scent of happy pheromones stirring their blood, and felt prickles of jealousy, quickly suppressed. I have no right to envy them. Both Hayle sisters have suffered long and terribly to find their happy endings.

I sigh and adjust my clawed feet on the stump, bits of crumbling, decayed wood giving way with rustling patter over the leaves below. Yes, I've suffered, too. But my lot has always been decided for me, my suffering orchestrated by those in power over me. Until recently. And now, here I am, expected to simply abandon two decades of training and indoctrination, and accept I'm no longer the servant, but the served?

Air snorts from my snout, puffs of mist cutting across my vision. I hadn't meant to think on these things tonight. This run was meant to clear my head, to be fun. I miss fun, as rare as it had been in my old life, it's even more precious now. Princess Sharlotta, heir to the werenation, must be sober and stoic, on the inside and the outside. But Charlotte Girard?

She's had her share of fun.

I shake my body, fur settling as I step off the stump and glide through the trees at a loping walk this time, unwilling to yet relinquish my werewolf form. I feel my most content in this shape, as though the woman I am is meant to be a beast, not a princess. But, I find at these times I most miss my old life. Never the one I lived before I met Sydlynn Hayle. No, it's the one that came after I long for.

I catch their scent before I spot them, drifting like ghosts through the trees toward me. The large, white female is in the lead, as usual, the pack Alpha, a handsome gray with a huge head and the bushiest tail of any wolf I've ever seen, close at her side. The pack leaders halt near me, their family spreading out behind them.

My muzzle vibrates as I growl a greeting and the lead pair rumble back a hello . I've never been able to fully communicate with them past a simple "how are you" and "goodbye", the language of wolves difficult for me in my were shape. But they don't seem to mind, my little pack, often tracking me down when I emerge from the palace to take a run.

They first made themselves known to me when I returned to the werecapital to accept the heir's throne, shortly after Syd healed us of the taint of the Black Soul sorcerers who created and controlled us. I scented the pack long before I met them that first time, a little nervous they might see me as their enemy, invading their territory.

But, from the moment they emerged to greet me, they have shown me nothing but curiosity and kindness.

The breeze picks up again, scent of a hot-blooded deer burning down my throat and firing my hunting instincts. The pack shifts as one, rising to their feet, waiting for me as though I am their real leader. I bow my upper body instead to the white female and her Alpha and growl for them to proceed.

Again I run, this time surrounded by the pack, feeling their heartbeats tied to mine, lost in the chase, the whisper of their paws over the ground, the sense of utter freedom and the savage need to run forever pounding like a drug through my veins. I could get lost in this, remain in my wereform forever and live among them, as one of them, content and blessed.

Sharlotta. His deep voice breaks my joy, brings me to a bounding halt. I watch the pack go on without me, heart now heavy, the white wolf pausing to turn, watch me as I wave her on with one paw.

Grandfather, I send, my tone as weighted as my corralled soul.

You're late, he sends in return, the sense of him on his throne powerful, the staleness of the indoor air he breathes choking me as I hold my ground and absorb the quiet night, saving up for later.

I look up at the moon, bark a soft curse into the air. The baby shower. Such an odd tradition my witch friends have, brought over from the normals they seem to do their best to avoid.

Ethpeal is here waiting for you, Oleksander sends with gentle admonishment in his mental voice, tied to the pressure of his disappointment. I cower where I stand, whining softly into the cold night air, a puppy chastised by her leader.

Forgive me. I spin and race at top speed back toward the palace, this run more frantic and erasing my excellent mood entirely. *I return at once.*

We will be waiting, he sends.

The final touch of his mind holds love and forgiveness, but not enough to salve the burning guilt now replacing my joy. I know better, that Ethpeal kindly agreed to come retrieve me and bring me to Wilding Springs so I can attend Meira's baby shower. And I'd forgotten, put my grandfather in an uncomfortable position.

Still berating myself for my selfishness, I cross the threshold of the trees and onto the broad lawn of the palace, the bright lights within beckoning me on.

About the author

Everything you need to know about me is in this one statement: I've wanted to be a writer since I was a little girl, and now I'm doing it. How cool is that, being able to follow your dream and make it reality? I've tried everything from university to college, graduating the second with a journalism diploma (I sucked at telling real stories), am part of an all-girl improv troupe (if you've never tried it, I highly recommend making things up as you go along as often as possible). I've even been in a Celtic girl band (some of our stuff is on YouTube!) and was an independent film maker. My life has been one creative thing after another—all leading me here, to writing books for a living.

Now with multiple series in happy publication, I live on beautiful and magical Prince Edward Island (I know you've heard of Anne of Green Gables) with my very patient husband and multitude of pets.

I love-love-love hearing from you! You can reach me (and I promise I'll message back) at patti@pattilarsen.com. And if you're eager for your next dose of Patti Larsen books (usually about one release a month) come join my mailing list! All the best up and coming, giveaways, contests and, of course, my observations on the world (aren't you just dying to know what I think about everything?) all in one place: http://smarturl.it/PattiLarsenEmail.

Last—but not least!—I hope you enjoyed what you read! Your happiness is my happiness. And I'd love to hear just what you thought. A review where you found this book would mean the world to me—reviews feed writers more than you will ever know. So, loved it (or not so much), **your honest review would make my day**. Thank you!

www.ingramcontent.com/pod-product-compliance
Lightning Source LLC
Chambersburg PA
CBHW070907180626
46817CB00003B/956